For seven years she'd pulled herself into a shell. She was sick and tired of hiding, of jumping at shadows. She wanted to confront life again.

All she had to do was reach for what she wanted most. Right now.

Caprice turned in his embrace. "What if I said I'd changed my mind?" she asked.

Luciano pulled back, eyes searching, assessing. "That's the shock of surviving danger talking."

"You don't feel it too?" she asked, her voice hoarse. "I feel it," she said, breathless. "I want you. Need you now. What more can I say?"

"Nothing. In the end you will expect more than that. An affair, commitment."

She shook her head. "Not anymore. No ties. No promises."

His eyes narrowed, and his hopes and desires soared. "You want my financial backing *and* sex?"

"Yes. We are bound together by a contract—there's no changing that. But when the job is finished so are we."

"Of course..."   and unreadable.

For as long as **Janette Kenny** can remember, plots and characters have taken up residence in her head. Her parents, both voracious readers, read her the classics when she was a child. That gave birth to a deep love of literature, and allowed her to travel to exotic locales—those found between the covers of books. Janette's artist mother encouraged her yen to write. As an adolescent she began creating cartoons featuring her dad as the hero, with plots that focused on the misadventures on their family farm, and she stuffed them in the nightly newspaper for him to find. To her frustration, her sketches paled in comparison with her captions.

Though she dabbled with articles, she didn't fully embrace her dream to write novels until years later, when she was a busy cosmetologist making a name for herself in her own salon. That was when she decided to write the type of stories she'd been reading—romances.

Once the writing bug bit, an incurable passion consumed her to create stories and people them. Still, it was seven more years and that many novels before she saw her first historical romance published. Now that she's also writing contemporary romances for Mills & Boon® she finally knows that a full-time career in writing is closer to reality.

Janette shares her home and free time with a chow-shepherd mix pup she rescued from the pound, who aspires to be a lap dog. She invites you to visit her website at www.jankenny.com and she loves to hear from readers—e-mail her at janette@jankenny.com

Recent titles by the same author:

INNOCENT OF HIS CLAIM
ILLEGITIMATE TYCOON *(Bad Blood)*
CAPTURED AND CROWNED
INNOCENT IN THE ITALIAN'S PASSION

BOUND BY THE ITALIAN'S CONTRACT

BY
JANETTE KENNY

MILLS
BOON

Published in Great Britain 2014
by Mills & Boon, an imprint of Harlequin (UK) Limited,
Eton House, 18-24 Paradise Road, Richmond, Surrey, TW9 1SR

© 2014 Janette Kenny

ISBN: 978 0 263 90874 9

Harlequin (UK) Limited's policy is to use papers that are natural,
renewable and recyclable products and made from wood grown in
sustainable forests. The logging and manufacturing processes conform
to the legal environmental regulations of the country of origin.

Printed and bound in Spain
by Blackprint CPI, Barcelona

BOUND BY THE ITALIAN'S CONTRACT

For Nick, my hero, my best friend.
You encouraged me to spread my wings and soar again.
I love you—yesterday, today and forever!

CHAPTER ONE

CAPRICE TREGORE WRAPPED her confidence around her like a protective cloak and strode into The Corbett, Aspen's newest five-star hotel, which a Russian billionaire had built one year ago to cater to the rich and famous. She surveyed the interior, her senses in overdrive.

It was a breathtaking, palatial design of marble pillars, gleaming granite floors and exquisite tapestries dressing massive walls. This lavish and elite winter hotspot was exactly what she had pointedly avoided the past seven years. If she didn't desperately need help, she wouldn't be setting foot in this playground for the rich and famous now.

She quickly circled the three-tiered castle fountain that dominated the center of the expansive lobby and scanned the myriad seating nooks tucked here and there for the handsome Italian she'd come here to meet. With rising annoyance, she realized not one man resembled him. Was he late? Had he stood her up?

"Punctual as always, Miss Tregore?"

That deep voice rumbling behind her, flavored with a distinct Italian accent, sent an electric shiver zinging through her. That was the last reaction she wanted this playboy to incite in her and she wouldn't tolerate another second of it!

"Punctuality is one of the cardinal business virtues,"

she said stiffly as she turned to face him with a professional smile she'd perfected.

For one second it threatened to slip as she stared into his riveting blue eyes framed in a face surely reserved for an archangel. Or the devil?

God knew either could apply to Luciano Duchelini. That reminder stiffened her spine and her resolve.

"A Don Marquis quotation, but you left the rest off," he said, not one iota of amusement ringing in that velvety voice that she'd once found incredibly attractive. "Always insist on it in your subordinates."

"I wasn't suggesting you were—"

"It doesn't matter. I watched you walk in five minutes ago," he said. "Your promptness is an asset."

That he knew exactly when she'd walked in the door spoke volumes. So did the fact he'd remained a bit hidden, making her seem the one a bit late and harried.

Not the impression she wanted to impart.

The Luciano she'd known had always run five to ten minutes late. It was a control thing and she'd accounted for it by arriving exactly on time. But he'd been here waiting.

That was a huge surprise. And a miscalculation on her part.

Seven years ago Luciano had been the world champion on the slopes, winning more gold medals than any Alpine skier before him, besting even his acclaimed father. The only things he was ever on time for were competitions.

It had been proven no man could beat him on the slopes. Rumors had flown that his ex-wife had captured his heart and taken it with her to her grave. That he no longer cared what anyone thought of him. That he lived for the moment, in sport and pleasure.

That no woman could reach the heart of the man.

Yet once she'd foolishly fallen for the champion, beset by a strong teenage crush. He was her idol. Her coach. *Her friend.* Or so she'd thought.

He'd used her friendship, her naïveté, just as he'd done with his lovers. She'd hated him then for hurting her, and hated herself now because she knew better than to trust his type.

He was a celebrated playboy. Life had been a game to him and he'd played it to the hilt. He laughed. He partied. He took nothing seriously.

Not her. She'd assumed the role of a reckless flirt one time in her life. A stupid act of retaliation that she'd regretted every day since. That one horrific incident convinced her that she wasn't a player in that world.

"Thank you for agreeing to meet with me," she said, refusing to let him fluster her.

He smiled, though it appeared as practiced as hers. "My pleasure."

If only she could say the same. She had to strike a winning deal. A position she deeply resented.

She'd worked hard. Saved. Scrimped. Yet it hadn't been enough to save her when crisis struck. Now she needed this deal or she would lose Tregore Lodge, her heritage, her home, her livelihood.

"I've come prepared, Mr. Duchelini," she said, getting right to the point.

He laughed, a brief, rich contralto that set his blue eyes twinkling and carved his beautifully sculpted lips into a half smile he likely used to charm ladies. "You are a take-charge woman. I remember how expertly you cracked the whip to get me to those pre-event meetings on time."

She nearly smiled until she recalled how bitterly their last working relationship had ended. "It would have been easier if you hadn't been a night owl."

He simply shrugged, just like he'd done back then only lacking the teasing smile. Zero contrition. She expected no less from a rich womanizer who'd skirted conventions all of his life.

"Come," he said. "Let's go someplace private to talk."

Said the spider to the fly? Being anywhere private with him was the last thing she wanted to do, but she said, "I'm ready."

"As am I. This way," he said, and gestured to the elevators.

She fell into step beside him and tamped down her annoyance that he hadn't simply arranged for her to meet him at a set location for their meeting. The sooner this phase was over, the better. No, not over. Resolved, so she could move forward achieving her dream.

"I brought plans for the lodge and a prospectus for my program, Mr. Duchelini," she said, not wishing to waste a minute, not wanting to be here any longer than necessary.

"Please, you know me. Call me Luciano or Luc." He motioned to the open elevator and she stepped inside, then stood as far from him as she could though she may as well have not bothered.

The mirrored wall behind made the space loom larger, but it did that to her companion as well. Not that he needed any physical enhancements.

Luciano simply consumed any space he was in with his commanding presence, absorbing the energy of everything around him.

She knew most women would be content to stare at his gorgeous body and classically handsome features because years ago she'd fallen under his charismatic spell. Not now, though it was tempting to admire him. Thank God she was stronger than that, that she'd learned from her mistakes.

"Very well, Luciano," she said, refusing to use his nickname as she'd once done. That would be too familiar. "To be honest, I'm surprised you didn't send someone in your stead."

He shot her a frown, his gaze cool. "There is much business that I attend to personally."

"You never used to, unless it pertained to competition," she said, and it was the truth. "What I meant was I hadn't expected you to fly halfway around the world to speak with me."

"It was no bother to coordinate my schedule to come here," he said matter-of-factly. "I was already in Denver to interview a ski therapist, like yourself, when my assistant phoned to let me know you were seeking a financial backer."

In a second, the stakes skyrocketed with competition thrown into an already tense equation, but she remained calm and determined to win his bid. "Good. I'm eager to discuss business."

"As am I," he said with a bite of impatience.

Game on. Having a rival meant she had one way to proceed—full tilt.

"Please," he said as the elevator door whispered open, motioning her to precede him with a disarming smile that was likely meant to throw her equilibrium askew.

Immune to his charms, she returned his smile with a cool one of her own and stepped from lift. And came up short. She blinked, surprised to be standing in a short hallway with a single door at one end and carved double doors to her right.

"This way." Luciano escorted her toward the double doors, where he reached around her, swiped a key in the slot and knuckled the door open. "I trust you don't mind discussing business in my suite?"

"Not at all," she said, stepping inside to regain the buffer of personal space he'd come too close to crossing.

The amazing view of the mountains from his private suite drew her to the windows. She welcomed the calm their rugged beauty always gave her, this grounding to reality that gave her strength.

"Thank you for showing interest in my proposal," she said, turning to face Luciano, whose attention seemed riveted to a small laptop open on the desk. "If there's anything in particular you wish to know about the designs I've envisioned for Tregore Lodge…"

"Your property is small and in need of intense restoration," he cut in, not bothering to look at her.

She cursed the flush burning her face, a show of emotion that she'd never learned to control. "True. Tregore Lodge needs major updating to make it competitive again. But I believe it has much potential…"

"I don't," he said, rudely shooting down the momentum she needed to build before she had a chance to explain how she could establish a state-of-the-art rehabilitation facility there.

"If you feel that way, then why did you ask for this meeting?" she asked, the question burning holes in her patience despite her determination to maintain a business mien, despite the determination to finance her program.

"Simple. The only admirable investment on your property is you."

"Is this some kind of joke?" she asked, needing to know she hadn't misunderstood him.

"Not at all." He studied her with eyes that took everything in and gave absolutely no emotion away, eyes that touched her as intimately as a caress, bold and without apology. "You hold my interest, Caprice. I want you."

Seven years ago she would have fallen all over him, deliriously happy. But then she'd been innocent. Trusting.

She knew better than to trust a man now. Though this was the faintest glimmer of the playboy she'd known, passionate and direct, she took his remark as an insult.

"Look, I came here to discuss business that is near and dear to my heart, Mr. Duchelini. If you're not interested in hearing my proposal, then you're not interested in me." She turned and strode toward the double doors with calm, precise steps, determined to walk out with her head held high and in charge of her life.

"Stay," he said, the command soft yet persuasive.

She stopped, fingers tightening around the leather handle of her bag. "Why should I?"

"I've a proposal that will benefit us both," he said. "I can grant you what you want."

That was a fact she knew all too well. And really, could she afford to walk out without hearing his offer? No, she admitted.

"Then let's hear it," she said, whirling to face him.

"With pleasure," he said crisply, then strode back toward his desk. "Would you care for a glass of wine?"

"No, thank you."

She never mixed alcohol with business, and that had never been more crucial than now. Despite his wicked reputation, Luciano Duchelini was a superb businessman, and he would expect the same of her. He could take advantage of her and her lodge if she wasn't careful.

Caprice crossed to the sofa angled near the balcony with her composure intact and her mind fixed fully on securing a means to fund her program. That was all she wanted from him.

"Tregore Lodge. Tell me your plans for it," he said, as he dropped onto a leather office chair and twirled it to face her, his long fingers draped casually over the curved chair arms.

"Gladly," she said as she set her portfolio beside her and dug inside it. "I plan to renovate Tregore Lodge inside and out. Foremost is establishing my alternative program for those who have never skied as well as for people who possess varying levels of aptitude on the slopes."

"Your program is tiered then?" he asked.

"In its most basic form, as you'll see by these," she said, her confidence snapping into rapier-sharp focus as she handed him a copy of her carefully prepared prospectus.

He lounged back on the chair and thumbed through the papers, looking relaxed and in charge, the last thing about him that was still organic. But he'd changed.

Not in looks or physique. He was still disarmingly handsome. Still lean and fit. But he'd lost all trace of the flirtatious, teasing charmer she'd remembered so well and adopted the image of a serious businessman who detested wasting his time.

Or maybe he simply still wasn't attracted to her. Maybe he believed if he was too friendly, he'd have a repeat of the teenager with the monstrous crush on the star athlete. If that was the case, he need not worry.

She had no desire in him beyond securing a business deal. "Regardless of one's ability, I slant the program to the individual's needs."

"Just what I wanted to hear," he said at last. "This is why I am interested in you."

"I'm flattered," she said, relieved he was referring to her program.

"As was intended," he said with a bow of his head. "Do you recall my brother?"

"Julian? Yes, I do." Quite well, in fact. "Years ago, he crashed often in your suite."

She'd immediately liked the boisterous Italian who took great pleasure needling and teasing his champion older brother. And the world had gloried in the upstart's daring exploits on the slopes, expecting Julian to set new world records, breaking those set by his father and Luciano despite his undisciplined ways.

But rumor had it Julian had kept his slot on the Italian team only because of his brother's lead position. Whether that was true or not she never knew. One month after the World Cup, Julian had broken his neck in a tragic ski accident and ended up bound to a wheelchair for life.

"Julian is lucky to be alive," she said and meant it.

He gave an abrupt nod, jaw snapping taut. "My brother doesn't think so."

"I'm not surprised. Paralysis is difficult for average patients to cope with. It tends to devastate top athletes." And Julian had been a new star on the horizon. "Recurrent bouts of depression are understandable in cases such as his. That is why adaptive skiing works," she said. "It boosts confidence both on and off the slopes, strengthens physical ability and agility, and provides a means to broaden social skills."

"Unfortunately Julian has gained less than desirable results with alternative skiing and given up the effort," he said. "Even more troubling, none of the therapists I've hired have a program as individualized as yours. He needs your help, Caprice. I believe he will respond to any challenge you put before him."

She blinked, his effusive praise at odds with his earlier criticism of her plans for her lodge. "Wait a minute. If you believe my program is that beneficial, then why are you hesitant to finance the renovation of Tregore Lodge?"

"It is too small a facility to sustain a program of your scope."

A fact she couldn't deny. Still, the lodge was hers and she could expand in time if she wished. "It's all I can manage." All she could afford.

"Alone, perhaps." He pushed to his feet and paced before the windows, his stride gracefully masculine. "You need to expand your scope. What you have envisioned has global appeal. Run with it."

He couldn't be serious. Just the idea of taking her program into the world market had her head spinning. She didn't want to run something that huge.

"You're talking incorporation and I want none of that," she said.

"Why?"

"I want the lodge to remain controllable, and I can do that by keeping it family oriented," she said.

He tapped one long finger on the side of his glass and studied her so long that dread lay like a lead ball in her stomach. "You want to police every aspect of your program. That's why you balk at courting the après-ski set. The expansion would be too great and you would have to delegate, to trust others, and you can't do that."

She stiffened, disliking that he thought her that intractable. "My reputation is on the line here. I don't want to slap my name on programs around the world, even if I personally train every therapist I hire. There is more to it than technique. The personal connection I strive to achieve with clients is what makes my program unique."

"Are you sure you aren't equating small with safe?" Luciano asked.

"I simply want to renovate my lodge into an alternative ski facility and launch my program," she repeated. "That's why I need a backer."

He pushed to his feet and crossed to the bar. "You want

my money and nothing more from me, and you don't want
to take a risk," he said over the clink of glasses.

"Basically, yes," she said. "Is that a problem?"

"It could be one for you." He strode toward the sofa with
two glasses of decadently red wine and handed one to her,
his gaze hot on hers, probing, assessing. "Everything has
risks to some degree."

Like being here alone with him. Like courting his interest and financial support, which was all she wanted
from him.

"I'm cautious, Luciano," she said, taking the wine at
last but hesitant to taste it.

Challenge glinted in his eyes. "Be bold."

"I am." *To a point.* "What's your proposal?" she asked,
mindful of the disastrous turn her life had taken the last
time she'd acted boldly.

"Ignite my brother's love of life again with your program. It is my hope that he will regain his desire to ski and
develop his own line of adaptive equipment."

All built under the la Duchi logo of course.

It was a logical sound business move that would surely
make Luciano millions. That he was going to great lengths
for his brother spoke volumes.

"I can't promise that therapy will totally heal him," she
said honestly. "Julian must want my help as well."

He sat on the sofa, so close to her she saw flecks of silver flare in his eyes. "Give him a reason to. In exchange
for your tireless effort and expertise, I will completely finance the renovation of Tregore Lodge to your specifica-
tions. Anything you want. Do we have a deal?"

She shook her head, refusing to agree to any verbal
agreement, no matter how tempting. "It can't be that simple. What's the catch?"

"No catch," he said, his gaze riveted on hers, hot and

intense. "I will finance the renovation and equipment for the launch of your adaptive ski program if you agree to come to my Alpine lodge and do all in your power to help Julian regain his life."

"Why is this so important to you?"

"He's my brother and has all but given up hope of having any normalcy of life," he said. "Look around. There are far too many like him similarly afflicted. I have the means to give him that new start. You have the knowledge to reach and motivate him."

She bit her lower lip, thinking. Her program would gain huge accolades if it helped Julian. But even if it didn't, she liked him and wanted to help. And she did need to cinch this deal with Luciano.

"What you're expecting of me is massive," she said. "The chance for failure is great. You must realize that."

His frown deepened but he gave an abrupt nod, troubled eyes meeting hers. And for a heartbeat she was lost in them. Lost in the emotional pain that flickered a nanosecond in his eyes before vanishing behind that same blank wall.

"I understand the risk," he said. "But it is worth it if Julian will one day lead a productive life again."

"That's admirable of you." Touching.

He shrugged, his blue eyes as turbulent as a restive sea. "As I said, I care about my brother."

She didn't doubt that. But something else was bothering him deeply. What was it?

This vulnerability of his to the travails of others was another change, a huge switch from the ruthless, competitive champion she remembered. Could a man change that much in seven years?

Her father had taught her that a leopard never changed its spots. Yet this stern businessman she faced now was nothing like the rash playboy she'd known. Nothing similar to the man she'd expected to deal with.

This Luciano was all business. Serious, driven, and clearly tormented. What had caused this transformation? His bitter divorce? The accident? Or did it run deeper than that?

Hard to guess as she rarely read anything about him in the tabloids either. It was as if he'd dropped out of sight. She rose from the sofa and walked to the stunning vista offered by the windows. She needed the space between them to think.

"Will Julian's transformation free you to live your life again?" she asked.

His jaw clenched. "My life is as I wish it. Your answer, Caprice," he said, his intense gaze locked with hers in silent challenge again.

She nodded, mentally kicking herself for getting sidetracked over the state of Luciano's health instead of getting on with her business with him. But she wasn't fool enough to accept his word at face value and snap up the chance to work with him, forgetting the slights.

"If we agree to this on paper, you've got a deal," she said and extended her hand just like she would to wrap up any business deal.

His lips curved in a rare smile that brought back memories of the fun-loving man she'd known. Just as quickly it vanished behind that wall of indifference that he wore so well.

"Excellent. I'll arrange for us to meet with my interior design team as soon as possible. Once they are made aware of what we require, they will be able to come up with a plan for my lodge by the end of next week."

"Whoa! I thought I was to decide how my program should be designed and implemented at your lodge."

"You'll have a voice at the meeting."

A voice she intended to use. "I suppose you plan to sit in on the design meeting for Tregore Lodge as well?"

"Of course I am. I'm financing it," he snapped, brows drawn in a dark frown. "Why are you being so contrary?"

"I don't mean to be difficult. It's just that this is all very important to me."

"Do you think it isn't for me as well?"

"I really don't know *what* you're thinking."

He muttered something she didn't catch, rose and strode toward her, his long legs moving with fluid grace, the broad width of his shoulders a shifting wall of lean muscle. Each step exuded power and masculine grace and purpose, like a cougar stalking the canyon rim in search of prey.

She stepped back, startled by the power that was all Luciano. He was a force to be reckoned with and she would do well to keep that in mind at all times.

He stopped, his larger hand grasping hers in a warm, but clipped shake. "I am thinking I made a very savvy deal with a very smart woman who I admire."

"Thank you," she said, pulling her hand back and hoping it didn't appear as if his touch disturbed her. "To our mutual success."

"It will be."

"You're that sure of yourself?"

His smile was brief but oh so cocky, just like the man. "I play to win, Caprice. In everything."

She nodded, not needing to be reminded of that. "This isn't a game to me either. It's business. It's what I've wanted to do for years and have put all my efforts into."

"Your business is your life," he said, his features hardening into a benign mask.

"I've put a lot of time into the lodge while my father was ill," she said, hoping he understood. "The past year it demanded most of my attention because my program is a fledgling operation and I couldn't afford a mistake."

"If you hope to succeed, you need to learn how to delegate," he said, advice she'd received before and ignored.

"Nobody knows my business like I do," she shot back in defense.

He frowned. "Still the same need for control, Caprice?"

If only this wasn't the first time she'd been accused of that, she thought, face burning. "I have to be picky when my reputation as a therapist is on the line."

One dark brow lifted. "You need to learn how to play the game."

That word again.

She had no doubts that he referred to business *and* pleasure, her heart kicking up its pace at the thought of the latter, which was totally unacceptable. Under no circumstances would she fall victim to his charm again.

So what if her business was her life? It was her choice, though she didn't expect him to understand what she had gone through to get where she was at now.

"I've told you before and I'll tell you again. This isn't a game to me, Luciano. This is my future. My dream. I couldn't have gotten this far with the few resources I have available if I hadn't focused on getting my program started," she said, gaze fixed on his.

He huffed a breath, shaking his head. "I do understand."

He couldn't. Not that it mattered. She wasn't looking for friendship with Luciano Duchelini. Wasn't looking for pity. All she needed, wanted, from him was a fat check for setting up her program in Italy and renovating Tregore Lodge before she returned to Colorado.

She needed his business acumen and financial support. Her best chance to get both was to remain immune to his charismatic charm as she solidified this deal. She couldn't let her judgment be clouded by emotions she had no intentions of pursuing.

"Where do you suggest I start delegating?" she asked, determined to move forward.

"Now. Let me be in charge of the renovations from start to finish," he said.

She stiffened at the idea of handing over control to him. "You don't want my input in my own lodge?"

"Your ideas are welcome," he said, though the impatience creeping back into his voice belied it. "But there is no need for you to remain in Colorado to oversee the project."

He was right. She couldn't devote full attention to her ski program if she had to deal with the building issues at the lodge. "You must understand that there are certain structural specifics I need in place to make my program work—"

"I get that," he interrupted, tossing his hands upward. "As I said before, you will sit down with my design team and list what is needed. When the plans are drawn up, you will see them again to ensure all your needs are met."

"I get final approval?"

"Of course."

She bit her lip, searching for a shadow to pick apart and finding none. "That sounds good." Perfect, actually.

"It is. I will bring this renovation of your lodge to fruition." He leaned forward, riveting gaze locked with hers, mesmerizing yet commanding. "Trust me."

"That's hard for me to do again."

He spread his arms wide. "Why? I was nothing but honest with you."

And he had been. It was she who'd raised her expectations.

My God, had she been that starved for love that she

had grasped for scraps? Was she still that emotionally deficient?

"I ended up hurt the last time I put my faith and trust in someone," she said simply. *By my mother first. By you, lastly.*

To her surprise, a ruddy flush streaked across his olive-hued cheekbones. "Believe me when I tell you I never intended to hurt you. I was—" he made a face, accented with a sharp upward jerk of one hand "—behaving abominably before the end. I regret hurting you, Caprice."

Dare she believe him? She wanted to continue thinking he didn't care about anything but himself.

Except that really wasn't true. He had come here to enlist her aid to turn his brother's life around. He was offering her a golden opportunity, albeit with him pulling all the strings.

"It doesn't matter," she said. Not now and it didn't. It couldn't.

"You have my word it won't happen again," he said.

She swallowed hard. Those were just the words she'd vowed to herself, with the added caveat to avoid Luciano's company. Now here she was, straddling the fence about taking his offer when she'd already decided this was her best bet. He was a genius at what he did. In that, she had to trust him.

"Then I will take you at your word," she said.

"Good." His magnetic eyes grew more intense. "The length of time the lodge is closed will depend on how long it will take you to establish your program at my Alpine facility as well as my brother's progress. A month is a generous estimate, considering Julian's manner of late."

She shook her head, saddened. "Julian may have appeared laid-back, but I remember him being a force of pure energy," she said. "He was always moving."

"People change, Caprice. My brother isn't the man you remember."

She would be stunned if the crippling fall *hadn't* changed the daring young skier. "I'm aware how an accident can affect an athlete physically and mentally. But I'm an optimist."

He stared at her, his features vague, unreadable. "I'm a realist. By proceeding with renovations here at top speed and avoiding problems, it will take at least two months to turn Tregore Lodge around."

Not what she wanted to hear, but there was nothing she could do to change it. Her lodge needed intense work and she needed Luciano's backing.

"I still intend to return to Colorado within a month when I'm finished with my part of our deal." She would find a friend to crash with until her lodge was completed.

"An aggressive prediction," he said, his intense scrutiny stretching the moment and her nerves to the max again. "The timeline doesn't matter to me. I want my brother to have the chance and drive to live life again."

"I'll do what I can to help him, but he must put forth the effort as well," she said.

"Therein lies the challenge." He shook his head, firm lips pressed in an unyielding line.

She blinked, unsure what to say. In her profession she had been quick to teach that a family member shouldn't set the bar so high. Each patient must enter into the rehabilitation process because they wanted change.

Whether that was the case or not, it boiled down to two things. She couldn't renovate her business without Luciano's help. Nor could she ignore this opportunity to help his brother.

Julian had been there for her once when she'd needed a friend, helping her get away quickly and quietly. She

owed him, at least in her mind. It was time to cease arguing with Luciano over minor points and repay his brother's kindness.

"Okay. When do we start?" she asked.

"Now. I'll get the team in place here, then we leave for
Italy immediately."

CHAPTER TWO

SHE WANTED HIM for his connections and his money.

Luc dug his fingers into the leather-covered steering wheel and shot Caprice a pointed glance. She perched beside him in his rented Mercedes, attention trained on the netbook on her lap, oblivious of his annoyance. And why should she pay him any mind?

She'd gotten exactly what she'd wanted from him—a financial backer with the added bonus of using his name and reputation in connection with her lodge. In that regard, she was just like Isabella, using him to better her own lot in life.

The comparison had him clenching his jaw so hard it ached.

Seven years ago he'd put Caprice from his mind for one reason. Her congratulatory kiss had stirred feelings in him that mirrored those he'd felt for Isabella. Feelings he'd buried with his wife and refused to ever revisit again.

Now that Caprice had reentered his life, the image of the bright-eyed young woman he clearly recalled was replaced by a determined businesswoman who sought to align with him for her own benefit. Nothing more, nothing less.

Strictly business. He got that. Understood it. Respected her for her drive.

He shouldn't find her attractive in the least. But he did.

It was her aloofness and passion for her program and her old lodge. That was the only plausible explanation for his fascination with her.

The only difference between Caprice and the score of women hoping to snare him into marriage was the simple fact she could help his brother. That was why he'd agreed to meet with her. That's the only reason why he didn't stop this car now and call the whole thing off.

He needed her to help Julian as much as she needed his money and the connections his name would lend to Tregore Lodge and her program. From a business stand-point, theirs was a win-win situation. As long as he kept her at arm's length, everything would be fine.

No problem, as she'd made it clear she wanted nothing personal to do with him. Their association was all busi-ness. Good. That's all he wanted from her as well.

As they headed toward the airport and Italy, she ap-peared content to immerse herself in her miniature laptop before the flurry of their combined work began. Unlike his previous traveling companions, she showed no interest in making small talk during the past three hours as they prepared to leave Colorado.

Not that he was complaining.

He just wanted to get home to Italy and back to busi-ness while she delved into doing what he'd hired her to do. With space between them, he could find peace of mind.

That was what he wanted. It remained to be seen if he would achieve it after putting himself through so much personal hell.

Caprice stared out the window, more frazzled over being secluded with Luciano than she was unnerved by the Den-ver traffic they whipped past. Seven years had passed since she'd spent this much time alone with a man.

She'd vowed never to leave herself vulnerable again. Yet here she was, traveling for over an hour with him. So close she could reach over and touch him.

Not that she would. Even if she had the desire to do so, there was absolutely nothing welcoming about his stern expression.

Which was just as well. Too much was riding on the success of their mutual deal for her to relax.

She wanted this job done as soon as possible. Only then could she return home.

If Tregore Lodge was still under construction, she would cope with the inconvenience. Heavens knew she had a lot of details to see to before the launch of her reno-vated facility and a return to total independence.

No matter what faced her in Italy, she *would* see it through. And really would her being in Luciano's com-pany again be that bad?

Difficult to guess, she decided as she stole a glance at him behind the wheel of the gleaming silver Mercedes he'd rented. As they reached the brighter lights leading to the airport, his deceptively relaxed pose was at odds with his hard-as-nails expression.

He'd always been demanding, a fact she attributed to his aggressive personality and his station. But he'd changed as well and she couldn't tell if it was for the better.

One thing was for sure, she would be right back in the thick of the elite world. Just like she was now, arriving at the private airport terminal in a rental car worth well over what she made in a year, scheduled to fly out on a private jet that cost at least a billion dollars.

He swerved to pass a slower car, and she noticed the imperceptible way he favored his right shoulder. Had he always done that?

At the lodge, she'd blamed his obvious discomfort on

the hurried way he'd loaded her baggage into the car. Now it was obvious his shoulder was bothering him.

"What's wrong?" she asked, noticing his chiseled features were more haggard under the flash of streetlights as he whizzed around the curved interior airport roads with the ease of a racing car driver.

"Nothing," was his clipped reply.

A lie, she was certain, if she'd read correctly that terse tone and body language that screamed pain. "Something is bothering you."

He wheeled into a parking space and cut her a scowl. "I have had very little sleep in nearly two days."

And lack of sleep had never bothered him before. But it clearly did now.

Luciano looked physically drained. Given his wicked reputation, she assumed it was from a combination of overindulgence and mental exertion while he was touring the U.S.

"How long have you been in Denver?" she asked.

"My plane landed at seven-thirty this morning, your time," he said.

She blinked. That only gave him four hours before their meeting, and he'd admitted to having an appointment before hers. "You flew here from Italy and went straight to a meeting?"

"I did not wish to waste time in the States."

That wasn't the Luciano she remembered. He was a party animal. The playboy who had the stamina to keep late hours and still perform with championship precision.

"Let me signal a skycap," she said as she followed him to the opened trunk of the Mercedes.

"Don't bother, I've got it." Yet, as he removed her bags, his movements seemed stiffer and his olive skin paled considerably.

She doubted his condition had anything to do with him loading her two suitcases into the rental and driving them to the Denver airport tonight. Nor was it the result of anything recent.

Under the brilliant glow cast by the private parking lot, she studied the lines of strain marring his handsome face, etching deep grooves around his piercing eyes and sensual mouth. Toss his terse attitude into the mix and it equaled a man who'd grown used to living with pain and hating it. Lingering pain. Reoccurring pain. Phantom pain.

She saw enough of it in her profession to be able to recognize it after a few minutes of observation. Luciano was gripped with the first two. Considering he'd been a world-class champion with a reputation for taking daring jumps and going at lightning speed down the slopes, it wasn't unusual it had left him with tangible scars from his years of fierce competition.

All of that abuse had come before the accident that had ended his career.

"I can read the signs, Luciano," she said, slinging her carry-on over her shoulder before he could add it to the wheeled cases he seemed intent on maneuvering alone. "The muscle in your left shoulder is cramped and the fingers of your right hand have gone numb, or at least they are in some sort of tingling paralysis. Right?"

He threw her a frown—no, a scowl befitting a warrior. "Again, my error is forgetting how perceptive you are."

She took the backhanded compliment with a smile. "It's my profession to recognize these problems with my patients."

"Which I am not," he said with a good deal of heat. "You've agreed to lend your professional services to my brother. He's the only Duchelini you will be attending."

"I wasn't offering to take you on as a client," she

snapped back, which wasn't true because if she could help him…oh, what did it matter? "I understand athletes detest showing weakness. The majority of them I've encountered consider pain from an injury a weakness to overcome. Am I right?"

"Yes," he hissed out. His long legs carried him across the drive toward the terminal with her two cases in tow. Then he stopped and cast her another impatient look. "Come on. The plane is waiting."

No surprise he wanted the subject dropped now, she thought as she beat him to the door and opened it for him, determined to have her say. "For one thing, you're wrong. Pain is not a weakness. Second thing—I believe you could benefit from therapy."

"I don't," he spat, every viral inch of him rigid with anger. "There is nothing that can be done to help me. Nothing."

The words plummeted like granite slabs on the concrete, shattering her tenuous confidence. She hadn't just touched the surface of a major sore spot with him. She'd raked over it with claws and flung salt into the wounds.

Crawling back into her protective shell and keeping her thoughts to herself would be smart. But she knew how the body reacted to pain, both physically and mentally. To a degree, she knew Luciano Duchelini—at least she knew the fiercely competitive athlete he had been.

"Okay. You've explored all avenues to alleviate your pain and nothing worked," she went on doggedly, just like she would with her patients. "But you've said it yourself. My program is different from the standard. If you utilized it to the fullest, there could be a chance for you to see physical improvement."

He bit off something in Italian, likely a curse aimed at

her. "Not enough to waste my time trying. I have learned to accept my limitations, Caprice. There is a difference."

"So that's it? You just give up?"

"This isn't about me. It's about Julian, and his injuries are life altering. All of the reports and reviews I've read about your program are glowing, and the professional techniques you've implemented are revolutionary. Focus on helping him with them." He motioned her inside, a muscle pulsing wildly in his jaw. "After you."

She looked away from his probing gaze and hurried through the doorway. Maybe he was right. Even with the best therapeutic programs out there, recovery from injuries hit a wall at some point. She knew that. Taught it often. So why was she pushing the issue with him? Why was she eager to discover his injuries?

The answer eluded her as she moved past him into the spacious waiting area of the airport with its welcoming chairs and scattering of passengers. She hadn't been here in fifteen years, but it hadn't changed except for an upgrade in the interior design.

She looked out the expanse of glass spanning the outer wall of the private concourse that lent a fabulous view of the private planes waiting to be boarded or disembarked by the rich or famous or a combination of both. The only time she'd been here was when she was twelve, and she was still haunted by the painful memory from her childhood leading up to that first trip to Denver.

She's of the age to be sent to boarding school, her mother's latest lover for the past six months had said one day as they'd readied for a trip to Jamaica.

Fine. Pay her tuition and I'll sign the papers, her mother had shot back.

She's not my daughter, he'd said. *Let her father assume her support or remain with her.*

And at that ultimatum, her mother had packed up Caprice and her possessions and flown to Colorado. She would never forget the shock twisting the reserved man's face when her mother marched her into Tregore Lodge, announced that Caprice was his daughter and ceremoniously dumped her into his care. She would never forget the sense of abandonment that haunted her still, despite the fact her father had accepted his responsibility and raised her well.

"This way," Luciano said, her body jolting as he pressed his right palm to her back.

For an insane moment, she wanted to lean into him. Wanted the heat radiating from his touch to melt the chill locked deep inside her. Wanted to feel needed and coddled just once in her life.

Sanity prevailed and she stumbled forward, breaking the odd hold. Already, being with him felt too familiar, too personal.

She moved to the aisle, walking slowly and purposefully when part of her screamed to run from the vortex of emotions swirling inside her. But there was no escape from memories, she knew as she continued toward the attendant standing by the door.

The woman's hungry gaze touched briefly on Caprice before devouring Luciano. The fact he always got that response from women didn't surprise her. The sudden tension and annoyance bubbling up inside her did, catching her unaware.

A denial screamed inside her brain. She wasn't jealous. She couldn't be. She wouldn't let herself be.

"Good evening, Mr. Duchelini," the attendant said in a soft purr. "Your plane is ready. If there's anything else I can do…"

"Grazie," he said, and pressed several bills in her hand.

The woman loosed a throaty laugh that set Caprice's

teeth on edge. "If you ever need another assistant for your fleet, or anything else," she added, stepping closer to him, "please let me know."

"I will bear that in mind," he said.

Caprice had no doubt that he would. There was never a shortage of willing, beautiful women in Luciano's world.

She took a step away from the pair only to be caught by a strong yet gentle hand on her arm. Her gaze lifted to his, questioning.

"We must leave," he said, his crushed-velvet voice warm against her ear.

She shivered, her breath catching in her throat. "Sure. Fine," she managed to get out.

In moments he hustled her across the tarmac to the waiting jet. This gleaming plane dwarfed the local charter ones she'd taken with the ski team from one regional airport to another. The Duchelini jet was close in size to the spacious connection planes she'd taken on short jaunts between major terminals.

"She was hot for you," she said.

"She was overtly forward and looking to feather her nest."

"I'm sure you're used to that," she said, well remembering that he'd always had a bevy of beauties at his beck and call, many literally hanging on his strong arms.

"The falseness? Yes," he said, his lip curling. "Women like that have their place, but I am done with them."

Which meant what exactly? She chose not to pry because she knew the type of woman he referred to, and because it was none of her business or concern.

She followed him to the skirted ramp rising to a gleaming white jet, the belly and tail embellished with vibrant swaths of red and blue that faded into a muted spray of color. The la Duchi logo, the same one she'd seen brandished on the most elite skis and winter gear worldwide.

Her stomach clenched as she gripped the rail and ran up the steps, palm gliding up the cool metal. A whisper of chilled air greeted her at the top.

Fragmented memories of her childhood flickered before her like a black-and-white movie, faces and names of people long forgotten or barely known. Nannies, the score of men her mother had romanced and the array of beautiful people who had played with their set in that glamorous world.

Caprice recalled few details, but remembered one thing perfectly clearly. She'd always felt alone in her mother's elite world.

Even now, there was loneliness deep in her.

The old uncertainty and fear closed in around her, holding her in the past. For a moment, she paused to take a breath and push those unpleasant memories from her mind.

She didn't doubt going with Luciano was the right thing, nor did she hold any more qualms over their business deal. Still, a second's hesitation needled over her skin, a last warning that the moment she stepped into the spacious Duchelini jet there would be no turning back.

"What is the matter now?" he asked, his breath warm on her nape, the press of his palm to her back, firm and hot, and stirring feelings in her that made her want so much more. Dangerous yearnings that she still hadn't been able to quell yet.

She didn't need the conflict of working closely with him. She was the professional here. She would find a way to cope.

"Nothing more than the initial shock of stepping into air-conditioning," she said, slamming the door on her past and childish longings.

She'd expected the interior to reflect a masculine and sterile tone. But the rich burgundy and cream seating, glass-topped walnut tables and warm lighting gave the cabin a welcoming feel. Like coming home after a long, tiring trip.

"Then I'll have Larissa bring you a wrap," he said with a beckoning curl of his fingers, and a trim woman with a kind face appeared from behind a curved wooden divider midcabin with a gorgeous pale cream blanket draped over her arm. "The cabin gets quite cool when we reach cruising speed."

"Thanks," she said, taking the offered wrap and moving to a plush swivel seat by the window.

Luciano strode to the stocked bar, his movements noticeably stiffer. Ice clinked in a glass, the sound loud in the spacious cabin.

"You should take something for the pain," she said to his broad back.

"I intend to. Bunnahabhain on the rocks."

"From Islay," she said, remembering his preferred Scotch.

He saluted her with a heavy goblet half filled with the amber liquor. "Do you still drink it or have you adopted a different taste?"

The fact he remembered she'd drank it at all stunned her, but she hid it well, just like she hid the dark moments of her life. His accurate memory was nothing more than an attempt at polite conversation.

"I did once." She couldn't lie to him because games had never been her style, her one attempt having ended disastrously. "Actually, I haven't tasted Scotch since Val d'Isère."

He studied her, features tight and unreadable. "You enjoyed it."

"At the time," she said. But she'd enjoyed his company as well. Far too much.

The week before he'd swept the events, they'd talked of their future plans in life, sitting alone by a fire sharing a Scotch. He'd never spoken of his ex-wife and she'd never summoned up the courage to ask.

She hadn't wished to sour his mood, immaturely sure they would finally cross the line between star athlete and volunteer. When he'd swept the events, she'd finally gotten the courage to kiss him with all the feelings bubbling in her heart.

And for a heartbeat he'd returned her affection. Then he'd cursed and pulled away from her, scowling, anger flaring like live embers in his eyes as he turned on a heel and stalked away from her.

Confusion and embarrassment had tumbled inside her like leaves caught in a wind. Rejection. Her first from a man, but far from the first time she'd been passed over.

Still, it had hurt and left her confused. When she'd finally gone after him, she'd found him lounging on a sofa in the bar with a beautiful woman in his arms, their lips locked together in a passionate kiss.

That's when she'd run from him with one intention—finding a means to ease the heartbreak.

"What's wrong?" he asked, the question jarring her from the past.

"Nothing," she said.

"You're lying."

She met his intense gaze with a spark of hostility. "I was thinking about the last time we shared a Scotch and how wretchedly it ended."

The muscle along his jaw snapped taut, which only fueled her own annoyance. Then, as now, she'd meant nothing to him, which was fine by her.

"What happened that made it such a bad memory?" he asked.

"You rebuffed my congratulatory kiss," she said, because that's what had started it.

What had happened after that would forever haunt her. Her dark secret.

He snorted. "That was not what your kiss implied."

"You can't know that." He couldn't have known she'd been wearing her heart on her sleeve. That she'd slowly fallen for him.

He nodded and splashed Scotch into two heavy glasses. "You were very young, Caprice. Nineteen?"

"Twenty." Barely.

"I did you a favor by walking away from you instead of taking you straight to my bed."

How different her life might have been if he only had. What was done was done. She couldn't change things now, but she could remember the lesson well.

"I'm sure you're right," she said.

He nodded. Frowned. "Now that we've settled that, will you join me for a Scotch? Or would you prefer something else?"

"No. Scotch is fine," she said as she took the heavy glass from him, the brush of their fingers jolting her again. This time she couldn't hide her flush.

He lifted one eyebrow. "Something else is bothering you."

"No. I'm just tired." She took a sip and caught her breath as the slightly spiced heavy liquor warmed her tongue and throat. "I forgot how good this was."

He smiled but kept his gaze on her, and the barely leashed energy pulsing between them had her tension strung high. "It will get better if you let it."

She blinked, unsure if he meant the liquor, this tenuous

rapport they struggled to hold on to, or something else, and chose to believe it was the former.

"Yes, I think it will, too," she said, trying for a similar nonchalance.

"Count on it." He finished his drink and poured another. Instead of taking himself off to a private location, he eased down into the chair across from her.

The rev of the jets increased and she felt the tiniest vibration just before the pilot's voice filled the cabin, the sound far less tinny than in a commercial airliner. "Ready when you are, sir."

"Get us home" was Luciano's reply as he snapped his seat belt into place, the la Duchi logo on the custom gold buckle screaming of the quiet wealth that was spent on details.

The interior lights lowered to an intimate glow for takeoff and the engines rumbled. She grabbed the burgundy strap and snapped her own belt into place, chancing another quick look at Luciano. His drawn features were more pronounced with his eyes pinched closed.

Concern welled inside her even stronger than before. He was obviously still in pain even after downing pain meds with two drinks that had likely packed a punch. At least the few mouthfuls she'd taken of her drink were making her head spin.

Even so, what he consumed hadn't been enough to affect him in the least. He was hurting inside, and her training told her it wasn't totally physical.

"What really happened that day on the mountain?" she asked, broaching the subject at last.

Silence roared over the monotone of the engines as the plane gained altitude, then leveled out, yet her stomach still felt suspended in midair. The details of that accident had been well hidden by the family. Why, she couldn't guess, but it was obvious Luciano wasn't eager to divulge anything.

"Luciano, I need to know everything in order to help Julian recover," she said when she couldn't stand the tense silence any longer. "There are psychological reasons as well as physical ones that impede recovery. If I can find a workaround for his internal obstacle, I stand a better chance of helping him." And Luciano as well?

Two champion brothers on skis. One horrific accident that had changed both their lives. Only they knew what had happened.

A muscle, or maybe a nerve, pulled hard in his cheek, puckering his olive skin. "The media provided a plausible version of our rescue and injuries."

She flinched, feeling the sting of his pain ricochet through her. Yes, she'd heard reports. Watched the news. Yet it was likely just what he'd said. A plausible version.

"Yes, I know where Julian and you were found, and I'm aware of the extent of his physical injures," she said, having hung on every word of the reports with the hope that Julian and Luciano would have full recoveries. "Now I need to understand the scope of your brother's psychological ones as well. The best place to start is knowing why two of the best skiers in the world chose to tackle one of the most hazardous runs in the Alps during less than hospitable conditions."

Luc drove his fingers through his hair and swore. How the hell could he satisfy her curiosity about the accident without revealing too much of his own emotional wounds? "It is the way of brothers who have spent their lives competing with each other in everything."

"There must be more to it than sibling rivalry."

There was. Too much baggage. Too much guilt.

He tossed back his drink and grimaced, hesitant to bear

his black soul to her. "Look, Julian is a Duchelini, second in line to a company that makes the best ski equipment in the world, youngest in a long line of Duchelini champions. It was a duty and privilege for him to compete in Alpine and win. Quitting was not an option."

"It was his choice to make."

"It was selfish, which is why Father froze his allowance," he said. "He thought when the money stopped, Julian would abandon his reckless bent and focus on the team."

"But that wasn't the case," she said, voice rising in question as she likely remembered how tensions had run high between the Duchelini brothers throughout the games.

"No. It was just the opposite, so Father charged me to intervene and get him back on track," he said, feeling removed from himself now, as if he were talking about a stranger instead of himself. "Julian was the reckless one without ties or obligations while I accepted my duty and became a champion skier and suitably married man with a day-to-day hand in the family business."

And perhaps he would have remained content in that role if his marriage hadn't crumbled in his hands.

"Did you resent your role?" she asked calmly reminding him of counselors he'd seen to no avail.

If she only knew the details, Luc thought sourly. But she couldn't and it wasn't a subject he wished to go into great detail.

"I did after my ex-wife died," he admitted, hungry for the punishment a free, grueling lifestyle promised.

She swallowed, going still. "You loved her."

"Very much so." He pressed his head against the seat, eyes closed as he allowed old memories and their pain to intrude. "With a bit of pressure, I was able to secure Julian a spot on the Italian ski team. But he didn't care about Alpine. Extreme ski drove him. Challenged him."

"Then why did he agree to participate in Alpine?"

"Father exerted his muscle," Luc said. "Adding to the pressure, the sports world jumped on Julian's natural ability, touting him as the faster and more daring Duchelini. It was a challenge few men could walk away from."

"Was he really that good?" she asked.

"Better than good. Off the record, he beat me most of the time." He fisted his hands on the chair, remembering how jealous he'd been of his brother's bravado and skill. His freedom. "All champions know it is a matter of time before their records will be broken. I shattered my father's records and Julian had the potential to best mine, but his heart remained in extreme ski, which is why he turned in such a poor performance at the World Cup."

"Is that why Julian seemed so upset the day I left?"

He leaned back in his chair and rubbed his knuckles along his jawline, glaring at the ceiling as the jet leveled off at cruising altitude. "No. I realized he got a tremendous high from extreme skiing and told him I, too, was going to compete against him there. He threw a fit. Said I wasn't prepared. That I hadn't practiced the quicksilver moves needed to attempt the extreme ski."

She wet her lips, eyes narrowed and breathing shallow, looking vulnerable, pensive, concerned. That last one got him in the gut like a blow.

"Why? You were a four-time Alpine champion, skilled in tackling the toughest slopes in ungodly conditions. At the World Cup I remember you attacking the slopes with reckless abandon, earning gold in everything you entered."

He loosed a bitter laugh at his carnal failings then and now, recalling that dark period in his life. If only he could alter time and go back, he might have been able to prevent the tragedy.

"Why doesn't matter," he said bitterly. "Alpine no longer thrilled me. But Julian refused to let up. So I challenged him to a race to decide my future. If he won, I would bow out of extreme ski."

"And if you won, you would compete against your brother in the sport he excelled in."

"Exactly. So I arranged the meet," he said, regretting the fool's bet every day.

"Wow." She blew out a breath, then another, and he only just stopped himself from reaching over to her, touching her, holding her. "Why did you pick the most treacherous slope in Austria for your challenge?"

"The Hahnenkamm was the best test of our abilities," he bit out. "I dreaded that mountain as most do and was grateful that winning my yearly race there was behind me. But it tests the best and that's what this challenge was about. Julian readily agreed, knowing it was beyond reckless to attempt it at the same time. But he lived to test himself and saw this as his means to best me."

"But he failed," she said softly.

He closed his eyes and watched that moment unfold in his memory, feeling the amazing rush, the choking fear and the crippling pain that never ended, that rolled on and on like a monster avalanche, clearing everything in its path. "He could have won."

"Then why didn't he?"

"It was my fault." He took a deep breath and huffed it out, gaze trained on the opaque wall but seeing nothing but blinding snow. Hearing nothing but the howl of the wind as he shot over the edge behind his brother and realized he was too low, that he hadn't launched off as Julian had. "I was behind him by a good twenty seconds when we took a dangerous jump. I miscalculated the distance and lost a ski and the race. And my brother—" He hung his head and broke off, swallowing hard, face carved in anguish.

"Don't go there," she said softly, reaching over to lay a hand on his clenched one.

He turned his arm and grabbed her hand, squeezing it like it was a lifeline. "He shouldn't have looked back. He should have kept flying down the mountain toward the next jump and proved he was the best. But he didn't. He ignored the most basic rule and glanced back at me sprawled in the snow. I looked up just as he skidded out of control and shot over the precipice."

"My God," she whispered as she laid her hand atop his arm. "You can't blame yourself for what happened."

"I can do anything I want."

"Let me help you—"

For one fleeting moment he wanted to accept her help. But that opened another avenue he wasn't about to travel with a good woman.

"Helping Julian will help me," he said, gruffly.

"There are other treatments—"

"No! What is done is done." He shook his head, accepting his penance, his guilt. "I have had surgeries, followed by long sessions with top physical therapists around the world. My rehabilitation dragged on for two years before I put an end to it. They can do no more."

"Are you always this intractable?"

"Stop being so optimistic," he said, and without giving her time to reply, he barked out, "I brought you to Italy to give Julian a chance at a fuller life. You're under contract do that and no more. In exchange, I will make sure you have an updated, state-of-the-art lodge for your therapy program in your quaint Colorado Rocky Mountains. Remember that."

"How could I ever forget?"

He hoped to hell she didn't. Hoped he could find that sweet spot that blinded him to the errors he'd made in the past. But then, in truth, he didn't want to ease the misery.

It was the penance he lived every day. His due.

Nothing would change that. Nothing.

CHAPTER THREE

THE MAN HAD absolutely no concept of failure, she fumed, welcoming the sleep that finally overtook her during the long flight.

At least it spared her from listening to any more of Luciano's vitriol. She'd made an error attempting to help him. Hadn't she learned years ago that he never wanted that of her?

Okay, fine. Lesson learned now. She would never again be the fool with that Italian who was clearly packing more baggage than a short line rail car. As he so clearly put it, she would finish her job and leave Italy as soon as possible. She silently swore not to give his physical pain, or a means to ease it, another thought as the plane finally touched down in Italy.

She pulled in a long breath, then another. For the next few weeks, possibly a month, she would need a surfeit of patience. If she focused on what she would gain, she could make it through this without a problem.

That thought stayed with her as they began the process of departing the plane and passing through customs. Thankfully it went so fast that Caprice barely had time to register she was standing on Italian soil before Luciano hustled her onto the tarmac.

"This way," he said, his features devoid of pain, his expression anxious, and then he was off.

She practically ran to keep marginally close to him, thanks to his long, sure strides. Obviously the long flight with scant physical activity benefited him. In fact she had to jog to stay behind his fast pace as he headed toward two chauffeur-driven sedans parked side by side.

Two cars? Did he mean for them to travel separately? God, she hoped so, having endured as much of his prickly company as she could tolerate.

But he was too far ahead for her to attempt asking, not that it really mattered. She was in for the long haul, no matter the discomfort.

Just before they reached the cars, the rear door on the one farthest away opened and a tall, elderly gentleman stepped out. He took a sentry stance, his strong features unreadable. Yet he was very recognizable to her, reflecting so much of the man ahead of her.

"Is it typical for your father to greet you at the airport?" she asked, finally coming abreast of him.

"Never." Luciano released a muffled curse and continued walking to the other sedan at a sedate pace that she could keep up with. "We haven't spoken in months."

"By choice or chance?"

"Both." He shook his head. "It's complicated."

A family state she knew intimately, she thought sourly. "I know what you mean."

His intense blue gaze swung to her, brow furrowed. "Do you?"

"I've been estranged from my mother for the bulk of my life," she admitted.

"You never told me."

"You never let us get that close," she said.

He stopped and grasped her hand, and just like that she

was gone, caught up in the river of fire gushing through her veins. She tried to block the power and pulse of him but failed, soaking him in like rain on the desert. And she hated the sensations as much as she thirsted on them, but finally managed to jerk free with a shaky smile.

"It's okay. I'm long over it." *And you.* Or was she? *Don't go there,* she told herself, focusing instead on what had shaped her. "When my dad passed away, my mother didn't bother to send me a note or flowers, or even call to check on my welfare."

"Perhaps she wasn't aware of his death."

"She knew," she said, not bothering to soften the bitterness that hardened her voice. "My mother is just as self-centered as she has always been. The day after my dad's funeral, she told the paparazzi she was out of sorts because her first husband had just passed on."

"She is a selfish woman."

"Very."

He nodded, walking at a more sedate pace toward the sedans again, tension radiating off him as hot as the heat rising from the asphalt tarmac. "You are nothing like her."

"That is the greatest compliment you could ever give me," she said, keeping stride with him as they headed toward his waiting father. "You don't know how much I envied people who had a normal family."

"Normal?" He snorted, the strong line of his jaw going taut. "Mine was far from it."

"Come on, you had a mother and father who were married and lived together. My God, you and Julian had everything money could buy. Even after your mother's death, you told me that your father ensured his sons got the very best education and opportunities available."

"True. But don't confuse a privileged lifestyle with a

perfect one," he said. "'Money can't buy happiness' is a very true saying."

A saying her mother would strongly disagree with. "I know."

They reached the sedan at the same time the elder Duchelini crossed to intercept them. Hard lines dug grooves into the older man's tanned features, but they merely enhanced his rugged good looks.

"Father," Luciano said, pulling her close. "This is Caprice Tregore, rehabilitation therapist extraordinaire."

Certainly not the tag she would add to her name, but it would embarrass her make to make a fuss out of his exaggerated praise. She managed a smile. "Hello."

"Good to meet you," Mr. Duchelini said, and lifted each hand in turn and bestowed a kiss on each. The gesture was so old and charming she couldn't take offense, yet she felt Luciano stiffening beside her. "Welcome to Italy. I hope your stay proves entertaining."

"Thank you, but this is a business trip for me," she said.

The older man frowned, looking from her to his son before landing on Luciano. "What is this?"

"Caprice will be setting up her program at our new lodge," Luciano said.

Again, she was treated to another exacting perusal from Luciano's father. "Ah, a beautiful woman and a smart one as well. A dangerous combination," he said to his son.

"Yes, she is," Luciano said.

And what was that supposed to mean? The only danger she saw was the powerful draw of Luciano that she constantly fought to ignore.

"What brings you here, Father?"

"A problem." His dark gaze swung to her, assessing she was certain. "If you will excuse us, I need a moment alone with my son."

"Certainly," she said and moved to get in the sedan, only to have Luciano open the door for her and offer an apologetic smile.

"This won't take long," he said.

"It's okay. Take your time." She busied herself fishing her netbook from her tote and hoped he didn't see how her hand shook.

Several strained seconds passed before the door closed. Only then did she take a breath and glance out the window. The two men squared off between the two sedans, looking obstinate and commanding. Father and son. So much alike in that regard yet something was driving them apart.

She didn't want to guess what it was. She didn't even want to know details. She only wanted to find a way she and Luciano could work together for the next month without tearing each other apart. And without her losing her heart to him all over again.

It wasn't going to be easy.

"What is this urgent business?" Luc asked his father, having no patience for this interruption to his own plans.

"Victore wants to do business with us at the new lodge. I can't refuse them."

"I can," Luc said with heat.

His father bit off a ripe curse. "Carlos Victore has been a friend of mine for fifty years. It would be a slap in the face to refuse to meet with his son because of past issues you have with Carlos's eldest son."

"Past issues?" Luc said, balling his fingers into fists. "His son had an affair with my wife while he was doing business with me. He's not to be trusted."

His father stared at him, unmoved. "Let it go."

"I most certainly will not let it go. I will *never* do business with a Victore."

And he most certainly would not stand here while his father tried to strong-arm him into dealing with the man who ruined his marriage. He stormed toward the waiting sedan.

"Wait," his father barked.

"I've nothing more to say on the subject. I'm considering Mario Godolphin as the architect." He wrenched open the car door and dropped in beside her. "Go," he told his driver as he reached for the door.

His father positioned himself in the door's opening and the driver noticed and remained parked. Stubborn old fool!

"Our families have done business for decades," his father said. "We are like family!"

"Family that stabs one another in the back," Luc spat.

His father slashed the air with a hand. "What proof do you have for such a claim? None, other than your wife and Carlos's eldest son dying in a horrific motor accident. Think, Luciano. We can make this work to our advantage. What do I tell Carlos and his son?"

"Tell them both to go to hell."

Luc pulled at the door and his father backed out of the way with a scowl that screamed retribution. He didn't want to have this talk and he sure as hell didn't want Caprice privy to the details of his family's scandal. "Drive."

The big sedan jolted forward, slamming Caprice against the plush cushions. Heat seeped from Luciano and tension pulsed inside the car. Her heart raced. Should she ask what was wrong? No. This wasn't her business. Wasn't her concern.

So why was her heart still pounding? Why were her fingers numb from clenching her hands together tightly?

"That was not pleasant," he said at last.

"Is there a problem with la Duchi?" she asked, the most logical thing that popped into her mind.

He barked a laugh that lacked humor. "My father wouldn't know one way or the other. He held a small figurehead role at la Duchi for years because of his impressive records and because my grandfather insisted on it. But Father's only gift was his supreme athletic ability regarding equipment design and an overload of *savoir faire*. As far as business acumen, he was doubly cursed."

"While you were blessed with all three," she said, genuinely meaning the compliment to the champion who'd come up with innovative designs and who could also run an empire.

"That blessing sometimes is a curse," he said.

"Everything has a price."

"Sometimes a price that pains us to pay."

"Do you want to talk about it?" she asked.

"No. There is nothing to discuss. I like my life the way it is," he said, his crisp tone and intent gaze on the road dissuading further comment.

"As do I," she said.

She had a home, business and profession all crammed into one. Her employees were trustworthy. Her few friends were loyal.

And so what if her love life was nonexistent? It was her choice. She'd never received any pleasure from a man.

Alone she was independent. In charge of her own fate and pleasure.

If she ever got the crazy idea to indulge in an intimacy, she would choose the time and place. She'd never let herself be victimized again.

And she wouldn't dream of entertaining close company with a man like Luciano Duchelini! When she'd known him years ago he had been an athlete at the top of his game. The champion. Arrogant beyond belief.

Everyone had wanted a piece of him, from the vast endorsements clambering for his approval to the women who hoped to win his heart. Even her, and look where that had got her.

Caprice pushed those dark memories again to the back of her head, preferring to let her gaze wander the land so very different from Colorado. Though they were on the southern perimeter of the Alps, well into Italy, place names were an intriguing mix of Italian and Germanic. Soft romantic sounds interspersed with hard guttural ones.

The mountains here were just as unyielding as the Rockies with bold limestone cliffs that screamed danger. Just like the man beside her.

He was the predator, a champion in winter sports and high-stakes business. She'd watched him dominate the slopes, and she was certain he attacked business with the same fierceness.

But she refused to let his bravado or his business prowess scare her into meek compliance. Though she never earned a medal, she did earn a degree. She was an expert in her field and was insulted by the fact he expected her to play by *his* rules.

He would soon learn that she refused to be the puppet dancing on his strings, she vowed as they reached the village close to an hour later. It looked more like an Alpine village than a ski area. The panoramic vista that seemed to stretch forever into the horizon literally took her breath away.

It was a hidden place of treacherous cliffs and lush hidden vales amid the backdrop of soaring snow-capped peaks. Shadows and amazing lights. Light and dark. Soft and hard. Like Luciano, who clearly had roots here.

Deep roots would be mandatory here. Clustered against the hills and nested on the flats were charming Alpine structures anointed with cream stucco walls and tiled roofs that gleamed a rich patina under an intense high mountain sun. It silently offered beauty and solitude. Yet for all its apparent quaintness an upbeat atmosphere pulsed in the air, as if the area were being prepped for an event.

Robust villagers waved as they passed, many shouting out warm greetings to Luciano, who returned each with a very broad, very relaxed smile that she'd never seen before. The transformation was miraculous. She blinked, certain she must have imagined the change in him from stoic traveling companion to congenial resident of this bustling settlement tucked in the Italian Alps.

Right now he was beyond handsome. Boyish. Open.

This was the man she'd caught a rare glimpse of years ago. A man she'd thought she shared much in common with. But she'd been wrong. She hadn't known him then and she certainly didn't know him now. Nor did she wish to.

The village might be a world apart from the après-ski scene she'd associated him with, but Luciano was the same cunning man. This show of relaxation was just another mask for him to don at will.

She wasn't about to be fooled by him this time. But she would give herself over to admiring this amazing village. Every building held its own Old World charm. Except for the mammoth glass and log structure that rose high above the village. The clouds shifted and rays of sun illuminated its soaring glass facade as well as the hints of dangerous runs streaking the surrounding mountains.

It was a curious combination of danger and opulence, just like the man beside her.

"Is that your lodge?" she asked, shielding her eyes as she pointed to it.

He slid on a pair of Louis Vuitton sunglasses, but the hint of a smile pulling at his mouth boasted pure pride. "Yes, that is la Duchi Royal."

Fingers of panic reached out to her from the shadows of her mind as he wound the car through the narrow cobbled streets toward the premier lodge overlooking the valley. She'd expected wealth unlike she'd ever seen before, but this went far beyond her imagination.

"It's fabulous." An understatement, but words failed her.

"It is unique." He glanced at her and smiled, and her heart did a crazy thump in her chest. "Like your program."

Her cheeks burned. "You don't have to keep saying that."

He shrugged. "It is the truth."

She tore her gaze from his and swallowed hard, shaken that his compliments affected her so deeply. Was she that needy for attention?

No. That was her mother's penchant.

She thrived on work and being totally independent. She had to be in control. Yet his compliments had begun to fluster her, and that wasn't normal.

Luciano was right. She was only comfortable when she was in control of her business and her life. Right now both were hanging in limbo, leaving her feeling on edge.

Once she immersed herself in this project, she would draw strength and confidence. She couldn't settle for any other outcome, no matter how much she was tempted.

Luc shook off the last of his tension like water and gave the sedan more gas, trying like hell to put the woman beside him from his mind. She was far too intriguing. Far too attractive, and that was a signal that he'd been away from his business for too long. But soon they'd be at the lodge and he could delve into much-needed work while Caprice did the same.

Apart. Maybe then he wouldn't be tempted to touch her. To see if her skin was as smooth as it looked, to explore how much of her well-toned body was tanned.

Seven years ago, her allure hadn't been that strong. He'd been able to resist her simply because she'd seemed more innocent. More playful. More inquisitive.

Now she was a woman in control. A very desirable woman. Far too tempting to him.

The last few hours he'd longed for sanctuary. If Caprice hadn't been with him, he would have whizzed past the exclusive lodge and hit the trail that wound higher to his private *rifugio* nestled on a mountain ledge.

But he would not take her to his hideaway. Besides, the luxury car would never make the journey and he wasn't about to stop to trade out vehicles. The designers were waiting for them to arrive for the meeting and that was what they would do.

As usual, he had no time for anything but business. But wasn't that what he wanted?

"The village isn't what I expected," she said, breaking the silence.

"And that would be?"

"Trendy. Busy," she said, nose wrinkling.

"A hotspot for tourists or more specifically, the haute rich," he said, taking a wild guess at her thoughts and sensing her discomfort.

"Yes. But it's just the opposite."

"It was planned that way to set it apart from the party havens," he said, quickly leaving the cluster of aged buildings behind. "Decades ago, my family chose to maintain the Old World charm of the village while keeping all the services up to date. They purchased the majority of the chalets, renovated them and hired full staffs. They immediately appealed to those who wanted exclusivity and were able to afford the cost of it. The village hasn't changed much in decades. The chalets are rarely unoccupied for more than two weeks out of the year."

"A getaway for the wealthy," she said, capturing a yawn with her palm. "Do you also own or hold interest in the local businesses as well?"

"Several are la Duchi holdings. They were bought up when the previous owners wished to sell," he said, hoping that put an end to her inquiry. "You are free to visit them after I give you a tour of the new facility and we have met with the designers."

"I'm anxious to see it and get started."

So was he, only for different reasons than hers, he suspected. "Good. We'll be there in a few moments."

She blinked. "You mean the meeting is now?"

"I told you we would meet the designers when we arrived here."

"Well, yes, I remember," she said and bit her lower lip.

"Is that a problem?"

"No," she said and sat up straighter. "But I haven't seen the place where you plan to house the therapy unit. After that I'll need a little time to gather my thoughts before I can discuss detailed designs. Even then, some things may need to be changed."

"I realize that," he said as he eased the car through the short tunnel to the arched portico where a valet waited. "We'll tour the area set aside for the therapy pod and go from there, if you have no objections."

She shook her head. "None at all."

Even though he had expected it of her, again she surprised him by being ready to dive in at a moment's notice. It was a trait that would suit her well in her business. A trait he admired.

He climbed out at the same time the valet jumped to open Caprice's door. By the time he'd rounded the hood, she'd fetched her bag from the trunk.

"If you please." He motioned for her to precede him though massive glass doors into the lobby.

"Thanks." She took half a dozen steps inside and stopped. "Wow."

He savored that moment, admiring her lovely backside before she turned, her eyes alight with pleasure, her gaze dancing over the native granite wall behind the bank of glass reception desks to the stand of trees that towered in the central rotunda.

"This is absolutely fabulous," she said, her face capturing her awe. "Who designed this?"

His chest swelled as he, too, surveyed the fluid modernity style that had already garnered three prestigious awards for the designer. "Valvechete of France. I commissioned him because my architect was off exploring some island in South America and I was too inpatient for him to return. Valvechete immediately stepped in and developed a design that was elegant yet fluid. Something that incorporated the location yet was innovative. In my opinion, this is by far his most stunning work. If not for my loyalty to my friend, I would use him exclusively for all my projects."

"Sometimes you just have to go with the better man," she said. "I've never seen anything remotely like this before. It's breathtaking."

"That was the idea." He made to press his hand to the inviting small of her back but stopped short. Touching her might ignite the need he'd so far managed to tamp down. Might suggest an intimacy to her that he definitely wasn't about to explore, even though he was sorely tempted. "Come. Let me show you the space allocated for your therapy program."

The short walk down the central corridor gave a commanding view of the valley, thanks to the walls of glass to their left. "It feels as if we are strolling along a mountain path," she said, face wreathed in a smile that erased the weariness he'd noticed earlier.

He ran his palm over the massive log wall to his right, proud of the rich patina it had developed over the past year. "I thought that would be a benefit to those who came here exclusively for therapy."

"Very clever," she said.

His face warmed uncomfortably. "Far from that."

She paused in the glass-walled rotunda to stare out on the ski village and the verdant valley below, the perfect picture to advertise the area. "I disagree. This view is riveting."

Not as captivating as her, he admitted. "Very much so."

He tore his gaze from her and focused on the mountain. When he built the lodge, he'd commissioned a top photographer to capture this vista from differing seasons, a job that had taken a year. But the end product had been worth the wait.

And yet for all its grandeur and appeal, owning this premier lodge failed to assuage the guilt that ate at him day and night. At times it actually made him feel worse.

"Time to tour the therapy pod," he said.

They walked side by side down the long corridor in silence. Sunlight spilled through the glass, brushing her hair with gold. Yet the excitement in her eyes was far brighter as she gazed out the expansive windows in turn.

"No matter where you look you see ski runs," she said.

"That's an enticement for those who come here for rehabilitation."

"It's good you feel the same way," he said, and this time
let her praise seep into him, allowing himself that pleasure. "The wider pistes are designed for alternative skiers.
The elevator off the therapy wing opens into their equipment room. From there, special lifts take them to the top
of the slopes."

"Your idea?" she asked, finally glancing back at him.

He shrugged. "It seemed logical."

"It is. Like the view from here."

He dipped his chin and smiled. "Do you approve?"

"Very much, but then as I said your design up to now
has been very clever indeed," she said. "I expect the pod
you've created for my program will live up to or exceed
that standard."

"If it doesn't," he said with a grin, "you will tell me."

"Oh, you can bet on it."

He had no doubts she would feel free to express her
opinion. That was what he wanted. Not someone who'd
agree to everything he suggested but someone who would
actually brainstorm with him to create the best possible
facility.

She was perfect for his needs. His wants. His desires,
he admitted, and tried to block out how much he desired
her as they crossed the glass-domed walkway specially
floored with a mat that absorbed sound as well as cush-
ioning one's step. When had she become such an alluring
woman? Why hadn't he seen this in her years ago? Or had
he and blacked it out because of his disastrous marriage?

No answers trotted forth. He knew better than to let a
woman's praise go to his head, even if hers was from a
professional standpoint.

"How long did it take you to see this completed?" she

asked, breaking the silence as they neared the glass doors at the end of the corridor.

"The major structures, lifts and runs took two years to finish." He glanced up at the mountain on which he once had loved to test his prowess and frowned. "Now it's time to add the final touches to it and take the facility to the next level."

For himself as well? No, he'd given up all thoughts of pursuing sports after the accident and had funneled his daredevil edge and drive into business. He wouldn't dwell on regrets either. But he vowed to open doors for his brother, and Caprice was the key he needed.

"You certainly couldn't charge exorbitant prices unless the facility was the best worldwide," she said.

He opened the pod door and motioned her to precede him. "Yes, it must make a profit, but as I told you before, I'm doing this for Julian."

She stopped a few feet into the room, her slender back to him. "That's noble, but I suspect there's a deeper reason besides brotherly love that drives you to do this." She faced him then, eyes questioning. "Care to share?"

He felt the tension snap through his shoulders, and knew she would keep picking away until she got to the truth. Perhaps it was best to tell her everything. "Knowing that it is my fault Julian is paralyzed, do you really need to ask?"

Caprice stared at him, seeming not to know what to say to that. "He accepted your challenge."

"Of course. He is a Duchelini."

She walked the length of the room in silence, the slap of her slender flats the only sound other than the rasp of his breath. Finally she faced him again.

"What does that mean? Duchelinis don't back down?"

He smiled. "It is a matter of pride."

"Pride." She shook her head and resumed her study of the massive pod. *"'Pride goeth before the fall.'"*

The old saying ricocheted off the walls and pierced his heart, drawing emotional blood. She had no idea how living with that knowledge pained him. No idea that seven years ago he'd pushed her away from him out of self-loathing because her kiss had touched on feelings he'd felt for his wife. Tender emotions that Isabella had shredded with her deceit. Stronger emotions because his wife's death had changed him.

Her death froze his heart and loosed a restless spirit.

Therein lied the regret that haunted him day and night.

The fall, as Caprice poetically put it, had severed his family in two. It had cut off any further efforts of his on the slopes.

After the fall, he'd given up what he loved because he'd lost all he loved. His unfaithful wife. His brother, as only a shell of a man seemed to survive.

His fingers fisted, his muscles tensing tightly down his side to taunt the injury that reminded him daily of his stupidity. His pride. Taunting him over what he could have had if he'd just been forgiving. As if staring into his brother's eyes weren't enough to scar him!

He ached to shout a biting comeback, but words failed him. At least cordial words. Not a single one came to mind.

"I'll leave you alone to decide what you need to present to the design team. Meet me in my office in an hour," he managed to bite out as he strode toward the open door without looking back to see her reaction.

What she thought didn't matter. This part of their planning would be done his way, and she would just have to deal with it.

CHAPTER FOUR

WITHOUT A DOUBT, Luciano Duchelini was the most infuriating man she had ever met. How dare he immediately haul her off the plane and expect her to formulate a workable plan for a state-of-the-art adaptive ski and rehabilitation facility that would bear her name. And on limited sleep at that!

Did he think he could best her? Or did he believe she really was that prepared to launch right into work off the plane?

The fact that was she semi ready was a major benefit. And that she wanted this job done as quickly as possible was another added incentive for her to focus on this instead of the promise of rest.

She could sleep when this job was finished.

With that in mind, she crossed to the bank of windows that opened to face the mountains and drank in the amazing view. Luciano had been wise choosing this wing for the therapy pod. She would give him that, and she would certainly optimize this vista that was key to her program's success.

It took twenty minutes to roughly sketch the placement of necessary equipment and another ten to adjust the initial list she'd used in her presentation package. A thorough edit and tweaking of minor details and she was ready to meet the design team.

If only she could say the same about being in Luciano's company again.

As she made her way to his office with five minutes to spare, she admitted that on a physical level, she was attracted to him. The unwelcome feeling grabbed her unbidden and caused her stomach to pinch tight.

She didn't know how to squash it. But she would.

The last thing she wanted or needed was a man in her life. Tolerating this stubborn Italian through the completion of their contract was all she ever wished to manage.

She paused outside his office suite and took several deep breaths. Game on. Affecting a smile, she pushed through the door. His secretary's head snapped up, the woman's attention switching from the neat stack of papers on the desk to her.

"Caprice Tregore to see Mr. Duchelini," she said

"Right on time," Luciano said, before the secretary could open her mouth.

Caprice whirled to find him standing in a doorway that had been closed a heartbeat ago, one broad shoulder propped against the doorjamb, perfectly sculpted lips pressed firmly together. Those intense eyes made one lazy sweep of her length, but this time there was something besides anger or challenge lighting his eyes.

A shiver of anticipation streaked through her, awakening that part of her that had slept for far too long. Pure animal attraction that she refused to act on, now or ever.

"Is the design team here?" she asked stiffly.

"No. Please, come in." He motioned her inside his office, but instead of stepping back to free the doorway, he stood like a sentinel with his back to the jamb.

If this was some tactic of his meant to intimidate her,

he had wasted his time and effort. She gripped her portfolio and squeezed past him, cursing him for his mulishness and hating how her nipples tightened.

"Where should I set up?" she asked, struggling with the nervous fear that kept her stomach queasy and her palms damp.

"To the left of my desk," he said, coming toward her. "Let me help you."

"Thanks, but I can manage."

He took the easel from her before she could stop him. "I didn't say you couldn't, but this way you will be ready in short order and time is of the essence."

Arguing with him would leave her in the wrong state of mind for giving the best presentation, and he did set it up in the ideal spot, so she bit her tongue and suffered his help in silence.

"Is there anything you need?" he asked.

A break from his close presence, which she knew wouldn't happen soon enough. "Nothing," she said and sent up a prayer as the door opened and his secretary poked her head in.

"Germaine and Fuseli are here to meet with you," the woman said.

"*Buono,*" Luciano said. "Send them in."

In moments, a dapper man and a tall, elegant woman joined them, the man toting an expensive portfolio while the woman clutched a netbook. Luciano quickly made introductions.

Caprice stepped forward and extended her hand toward the elder of the pair, making it clear she wished to take charge of her program. If Luciano took offense at her boldness, he certainly masked it well. In fact, he appeared as eager as her to get past this phase.

"Nice to meet you both," Caprice said. "Luciano promised you were the best designers for my program."

"We strive to please," Mr. Fuseli said, and his partner nodded in agreement.

"Which you do to perfection," Luciano said to the designers. "Caprice has developed a unique and amazing program. It is up to you two to determine her needs so this facility exceeds her expectations."

"We're ready whenever Ms. Tregore is," Ms. Germaine said, her accent bearing a hint of French.

Caprice looked for a place to sit that was far from Luciano and his desk. Too late, his gaze snared hers again, and this time she felt the burn of desire scorch her soul. Curse him for doing this to her now when she needed to be on.

She tore her gaze away and settled on a stuffed chair in the sitting area that gave an enviable view of a startlingly challenging ski run. Pushing him from her mind, she fetched her notebook from her bag, all the while mentally reviewing her specific needs. A few clicks and she pulled up the file that detailed her program. "I'm ready."

"Excellent," Mr. Fuseli said and nodded to the elegant Ms. Germaine, who immediately began shooting her questions.

Twenty minutes later Caprice had answered them all. She ended by handing them rough sketches for the placement of equipment and a furnishing list.

The designers huddled together to review her drawings. Germaine shot her an excited smile. "I can see this in grays and blacks highlighted with reds and glass."

"Yes, it is perfect for a European theme with clean lines. Monochromatic with the occasional splash of intense color to define," Fuseli chimed in. "We can have a fully scaled mock-up done in a week for your approval."

"Nothing sooner?" Caprice asked.

Fuseli stroked his narrow chin with thumb and forefinger. "Perhaps by a day."

"And if I don't care for this design?" Caprice asked.

Luciano threw his hands in the air. "You will. But if you don't, then they will produce another for your perusal."

"That's all well and good except for the fact we'll fall another week behind schedule while the designers create a new mock-up." Which meant she would be in Luciano's company that much longer.

Ms. Germaine frowned, glancing at Luciano. "If time is crucial, then why don't you show her your *rifugio*?"

"Yes, yes, good question. That design is exactly what we envision for here. But perhaps you've sold the property," Fuseli quickly added.

Luciano stiffened. "I haven't sold it, but taking Miss Tregore there is out of the question."

The designers nodded, but Caprice could only stare at Luciano. Why was he balking at showing her the design? Whatever the reason, she wouldn't have it.

"Luciano, could I have a moment alone with you before we go any further?" she asked.

He fixed a cool stare on her, his blue eyes snapping with irritation. "Is this necessary?"

"Only if you expect me to proceed with the program."

His jawline hardened, but he gave a nod and addressed the pair. "If you please, would you mind stepping into the outer office for moment?"

"Not at all," Fuseli said, and the pair hurried out, closing the door in their wake.

"Do they seriously expect me to copy a known design of yours?" she asked, keeping her voice low.

"This is *my* design and is known only to a select few that have seen my *rifugio*," he said dismissively.

She frowned, her muzzy mind struggling to grasp the

meaning of the word, but the way it rolled off his tongue
made the place sound sensual and relaxed. Intimate. Exactly the place she never wished to go with him.

"How far is it from here?"

"A day's journey and back at the most," he said, irritation sharpening his words. "Why do you ask?"

"I want to see it."

"Out of the question."

She bracketed her hands on her hips. "Why? What is
this place?"

"It was an old refuge for shepherds and skiers caught
out in inclement weather, built just below the snowline
like all the *rifugios* that dot the Dolomites. I've turned it
into my private retreat."

A hideaway. "On the order of Rocky Mountain line cabins," she said more to herself, becoming less convinced
anything remotely similar to that would suit her needs.
"What makes you so sure I will like the design?"

"I paid attention to your body language when we met
in Denver, while we were at your lodge and when we arrived here as well. I listened as you talked with the designers about what you wanted. You've yet to feel totally
comfortable," he said.

She wanted to dispute him but couldn't. "You're right.
I want a plan that is clean and open, but I don't want stark
modernism, nor do I want classic elegance, or Western
themed."

"As I thought. You wish to keep the integrity of your
historic old lodge, yet you don't want the interior to be
rustic, ultra-modern or lavish."

He was trying to sell her on a design sight unseen, but
she wasn't about to cave in. Time was too crucial.

"Am I right?" he pressed.

"Yes."

He smiled. "Good. May I bring the designers back in so we can finish this?"

"Please do."

Stay strong! The only way she knew how to do that was to take control now before this totally spiraled out of hand.

"You are all convinced I will love this design done at the *rifugio*. Correct?" Caprice asked when the designers stepped back into the office.

The designers nodded, but Luciano raised a questioning brow. "Caprice," he said in a warning tone.

But she ignored him and pressed on. "Then I insist we save time and energy. Take me to the *rifugio*."

"Splendid idea," Ms. Germaine said, gaining a nod of approval from her partner. "We shall still start the second design idea, but will await your approval on the first. You are both in agreement?"

"Well?" Caprice asked, arms crossed over her bosom, joining the designers to stare at Luciano.

His chest heaved and his blue eyes went black. "You insist on seeing it? Fine," he said, throwing his hands in the air for the second, or perhaps third time, and the designers quickly left, leaving her alone with a very irate, very intense Italian.

She took a steadying breath and blew it out, determined to see this through, well knowing the consequences and the chances to gain. Her mind was set. Do-or-die time. She wanted this over and done with.

"When do we leave?" Caprice asked.

He combed his fingers through his hair and paced the room, clearly agitated. "I will take you there tomorrow."

"Why waste the time? Can't someone take me now?" she pressed, aware she was pushing him, aware this could go badly for her as it had the last time she'd pushed buttons she had no business pushing.

He whirled and stalked toward her, clearly furious. Panic nipped along her nerves, touching on old fears. She tried slipping behind the protection of the divan, but she wasn't quick enough.

His big palms cupped her cheeks and her mind fizzed like champagne uncorked too quickly. Panic bubbled in her as well and she grasped his wrists, her gaze meeting his. And her tension popped, her fears gearing down to nothing. This was Luciano, the man she'd shared a room with sans sex. The man who was financing her dream. The man who'd moved the mountain of doubts and fears in her far too easily, expecting only one thing she was certain of—her compliance.

Easily won right now because she could drown in those fathomless blue eyes. If she let herself...

"Caprice, my *rifugio* is on a high, remote step to the north of us," he said in a gruff voice that feathered along her skin. "It is near the Austrian border and will take an hour over a rough track to get there."

She swallowed hard, debating the wisdom of spending the rest of the afternoon with him, especially as she knew how much his nearness affected her. How weak she could be with him if she let go. And that was the key. She couldn't let go. She had to keep pushing forward, pushing hard for what she wanted. What she believed herself capable of doing.

What better reason could there be for wanting to take this reckless course?

None. At least not for her.

The longer she dawdled here following Luciano's relaxed schedule, the more personal torment she would endure. She looked toward the day that she would put a period on this project and walk away with her head held proud. She would not slink off in the night as she'd done before.

"It's still early, right?" she said, carefully extracting

herself from his light hold to glance at the clock, pretending she was totally unaffected by him. "So if we leave now, it'll take an hour to drive up. Even if we waste thirty minutes there, we would still be back at la Duchi Royal before five p.m."

He snorted. "I don't want to hear any complaints about the bumpy drive."

"Hey, I grew up in the rugged Rockies. Rough mountains tracks and roads are home to me," she said, meaning it.

"You're sure of this?"

"Positive." Never mind that it all sounded heavenly and inviting and far too dangerous a place to be secluded with him.

"Fine. We'll go now."

He ushered her out the door without ceremony toward his private elevator. Yet as the door swished open and she stepped inside, she felt his power throb and grow, felt the pulse of the man beating in her veins as well. Her heart pounded in rhythm and felt expectation ripple through her.

How stupid could she get! Luciano was nothing more than her business associate. Old friend. Never lover. Never. She willed that vow to embed itself in her mind and sucked in air, but that only drew the spicy scent of him deeper into her lungs and her blood.

"Are you all right?" he asked.

She feared she'd never be all right again, but nodded. "I'm just anxious to see the design of your *rifugio*." Anxious to get this leg over with, return to the lodge and have a moment's peace without Luciano.

"Soon."

Having dressed in appropriate gear, they arrived in a garage lined with a dazzling array of cars, all high octane and high dollar, she was certain.

Instead of going for the sedan they'd arrived in or the Land Rover, he ducked his head under the open canopy and swung his long, muscled leg over the black padded seat of an impressively large all-terrain vehicle. "Climb on. I would prefer getting there before it turns dark or storms."

She looked at the sky and shivered. Though a good distance from them, a dark cloud bank was moments away from blocking out the sun and her avenue of daylight.

Being in the mountains after dark didn't bother her nearly as much as the thought of getting caught out in bad weather. His handsome face, carved in impatient lines with a critical inspection of the rugged ATV tires, got her moving forward. She swung on behind him just as he fired up the powerful engine, sending an unsettling vibration through her nerves and her blood that she had so longed for.

"Is anything wrong?"

"Nothing. Hang on," came his clipped order as he shifted gears and backed them from the massive garage.

Caprice spent a millisecond running her palms down the passenger grab bars before she pressed her spine against the plush seat back. The war between hanging on to to the bars or simply relishing reckless freedom darted within her.

Luciano barked an order. "Buckle up or hang on."

His muscled physique was inviting. Too inviting.

She fastened the black web belt over her flat belly with a snap because she wasn't about to wrap her arms around him. No matter the allure. No matter how much a part of her wanted to touch him, feel him, taste him. She wasn't about to do any of that.

He gave her one quick look back before he sent the ATV in motion and took a trail that wound above the massive manicured lawn of the lodge to a rugged track that angled away from the ski village. The harsh beauty of the mountains called to her soul while the sensual pulse of the man before her threatened to tempt her heart.

In what seemed like moments, the ATV swerved and jolted up the uneven mountain trail that ran parallel to a rushing stream littered with rocks, climbing higher at an angle that took them so far from the ski village she couldn't even see those roofs now. Each yard they traveled threatened to slam her against his broad back. She resisted, staying strong. Away from him.

The air was thinner at this elevation and deep snow still hid in crevices and shadowed nooks on the northern slopes high above the trail. Really, it was similar to the terrain in Colorado, where hearty trees struggled for survival on the unforgiving terrain of rocks and soil. The occasional alteration in the track below bore swaths that screamed danger, clear evidence of massive slides of soil and rock likely brought down the slope by heavy slabs of snow.

Her unease compounded as the wind tormented her with his spicy scent, forcing her to breathe him in with each breath she took, to feel the man on her skin and in her blood. The uneven terrain conspired against her battle to keep a careful distance.

"Hold on. It gets rough for the next few kilometers," he said after they'd been on the trail a good thirty minutes.

Halfway point, she hoped. Yet this was an exhilarating slice of heaven she wouldn't have wanted to miss. The vistas were incredible, dwarfing the Rockies with their beauty.

Just as she was getting into her stride the heavy ATV busted over the uneven track with another, larger, bared slope rising to the summit. Clearly a small avalanche had scrubbed a narrow pathway, leaving gullies and massive boulders clinging to the face. The ATV bucked and sprayed gravel, sand and slush in a rooster's fantail that covered their trail over this rugged patch. Then the route evened with thick trees on the slope and a swift running stream to their right.

On the other side of the stream rose a smaller ledge of firs that flattened out into a dense stand of trees. It made the area they traveled more a wedge of safety than a valley, and by no means eliminated them from danger. In fact she couldn't imagine this route being used at all during the winter months. Isolated? Chillingly so, she thought on a shiver.

A mile or perhaps more up the winding rising track, the surface turned dangerously rocky. Luciano geared down and took it slower over the track, which rose unevenly. Instinctively she looked up the towering slope to the slab of deep snow suspended in above them, stretching across the face near the summit.

"Has it been cool here?" she asked in a near shout.

She felt him tense and peer up the slope as well. "It had been, but my groundsman alerted me to the sudden spike in temperatures yesterday and today, coupled with above-freezing numbers at the summit."

Her stomach clenched painfully, her heart kicking up pace. "Avalanche danger."

"It's a possibility," he said. "That is why I was hesitant to come up here today."

It wouldn't take much for that ridge of snow to turn deadly. Above-freezing temperatures at night. Hot days. Rain. Any combination could send that mass of ice and slush tumbling down the slope, wiping out everything in its path.

"Why didn't you say so at the lodge?" she asked.

He snorted. "*You* wanted this done with, and I do as well."

Was she that transparent to him? Was he that anxious to be free of her?

Her palms skimmed over the grab bars until a burst of speed up the tree-lined track jolted her. She wrapped her arms around his lean waist and leaned against his strong back. Cooler air buffeted her face and back while the heat of the man seeped into her length.

"Hang on. We're almost there. See the green roof on the far ledge?" he shouted over the rev of the engine that tormented the tender flesh between her legs in a sinfully delicious way. "That is my *rifugio*."

She caught a glimpse of the chalet-like structure before the winding trail took the ATV speeding down a sharp, curving dip in the trail. She buried her face against his broad back for a millisecond, then looked up.

Excitement hummed through her, her heart accelerating with each rev of the engine that gave a sensual jolt of her body against his broad back. Feeling his muscles tighten was a delicious torment that she had never felt on a pleasurable level, but she wanted more, wanted to explore those feelings.

Don't pursue it, the rational part of her brain warned as the ATV all but crawled over the rough track, the dips and jolts creating a delicious torture she hadn't anticipated.

A sound like thunder turned her blood cold and yanked her attention from the man to the mountain. Snow sprayed over a high ledge into the air, quickly tumbling downward. The wide surf of tumbling, sliding white snow flung rocks ahead of it, the mass turning browner as it gathered more snow, soil and trees. A new fear skittered up her spine.

"Avalanche!" she screamed.

"Hang on," he ordered at the same time as he boosted the ATV to a reckless speed.

She splayed her fingers on his chest and held tight, heart

pounding in rapid tandem with the beat of his against her palm. The roar up the slope increased and a glance up proved the snow slide was gaining more speed than they were. My God, they'd get eaten alive by the snow.

"Go faster," she implored.

"We're at top speed now," he shouted back.

Not fast enough. That realization played over and over in her mind, a litany of doom to come. One by one, the trees disappeared under a wall of snow and soil, the crack and splintering louder than violent cracks of lightning over the hum and rev of the ATV. Massive boulders vanished, torn from their mooring of earth only to shoot out amid sprays of ice and dirt ahead of the wall of dirty white, tumbling into a hellish maelstrom that raced toward them.

"Can we outrun it?" she gasped, holding on to him for dear life, heart in her throat.

He flicked a glance back at the deathly gray slope, blue eyes hard as flint and tinged with terror. "I hope to hell so. If not…"

She knew from her last glance that the horrendous slide was too close. The tumbling tide of snow in front of the avalanche was less than twenty feet from engulfing them and gaining fast. Too fast. A glance ahead had her guessing how far they were from the safe zone.

They had a fifty-fifty chance. *If that much.*

The fear and horror of her past paled in comparison to this horror. No terror compared to the nanosecond the spray slammed into them, tossing them off track.

Luciano spat a curse and the ATV revved and roared, swerving and bucking for a heart-stopping moment. She couldn't make out any details, not even the man she clung to. Snow and mud rained down on them, soaking her with muck and fear. Stones pummeled her head, her back so much she wanted to scream out the pain.

Somewhere came the crash of snow and trees. Deafening deadly sounds. Ice pellets pounded her back and arms and head. It soaked her in seconds, matting her hair to her head. Each labored breath was torture.

Something hard, a limb, or perhaps rocks slammed into the back of the ATV. She whimpered, eyes blurring, at the same time Luciano swore violently. Her fingers scrambled to find purchase on his soaked clothes, her head spinning and aching.

Tired. She was so damned tired of clinging to him. And afraid, more than she'd ever been in her life. Their chances of outrunning an avalanche had been slim. Surviving one was a rarity.

"Hold tight!" Luciano shouted.

She jerked and did just that, plastering herself against his broad back, knowing he was taking the brunt of the fallout, wildly thinking this was what clothes felt like tossed in a washing machine. Soaked. Wrung out. Limp.

She took a breath and gagged. Tasted the mud on her lips.

The ATV engine whined and roared, shooting them through a wall of muck that blinded her. The tight pinch to her stomach and heightened rev of the engine told her they'd propelled into the air. Into what? Would they get buried under a massive drift of snow-covered debris? Would the force slam them into boulders or the jagged ledge? Or would they end up propelled over the mountain's edge?

Was death imminent? Was this her last moment?

She didn't want to die. Didn't want Luciano to either. Didn't want either of them hurt. But it was out of her hands and his.

Please, God, she prayed. *Please!*

The ATV dropped with a jolt and reared, but somehow

Luciano kept it speeding forward. She swallowed a scream and clung to him, unable to see anything ahead of them under the pummeling waterfall of snow and mud.

In a blink they shot out into open space.

She swiped at the grime on her face and stared ahead. Fingers of tumbling snow and debris reached ahead of them. Further ahead were whole trees and unspoiled land. Was safety that close?

The promise of escape barely registered before the ATV plunged into a roiling finger of snow and debris. She cringed as her body was peppered again with God knew what. Inside that maelstrom she couldn't even see Luciano before her, yet she felt his muscles bunch and clamp down as the ATV tipped on its rear axel. She clung to him over the manic rev of the engine and wheels spinning frantically without purchase. Crashing was imminent and her hands were so sore and slickened by snow and sludge that she could barely hang on.

The debris tormented them for long seconds that felt like hours before the ATV rocketed out from the far fringe of the avalanche tide. The unspoiled track and treed slope she'd glimpsed before was right ahead. Was she dreaming? Had they survived?

Luciano maneuvered the ATV between a tight stand of trees, dropping down and away from the ledge of snow. Something about the surety of man in the face of danger called to her as nothing else ever had.

It was comforting. Strengthening. Seductive.

Danger pulsed in her heart and cried in her soul, danger that had everything to do with nearly losing her life and her heart to this bold, reckless man. She didn't want either to happen, but she'd never felt this heart-stopping adrenaline rush before.

The ATV sped up the trail along the sloped woods. She

held tight to the grab bars with hands that were near numb and peered over her shoulder at the cascading tumble of snow and debris that still raced down the slope. The heart of the avalanche bulldozed across the track they'd narrowly just traveled and dumped into the stream in a mixture of muck mingled with boulders and trees torn from the earth.

In seconds, the trail was blocked, she realized with a sinking heart as the area between the slope and the ridge beyond the stream filled in, burying the trail and damming the stream.

Her breath came short and fast, and her heart thundered in her chest. They'd barely escaped getting buried alive beneath a mountain of earth, stones and crusted snow. They'd cheated death. But how would they get back to the village?

Luciano pulled to a stop at the hillocks summit and swung off the ATV, his breathing labored and eyes unnaturally bright. "All you all right?"

All right? No, she was far from it, but she nodded anyway and got off barely standing on shaky legs, her entire body still riding the wave of charged danger.

It was preternaturally quiet. "Is it over?"

"That one is," he said, staring at the mountains with critical eyes.

She wanted to cry. Wanted to give up, but she did neither. They were alive. Wet. Filthy. Cold. But alive.

He pulled a blanket from the small boot on the ATV and wrapped it around her without ceremony. "You're shivering."

"So are you," she said and clutched the blanket under her chin. "Thank you."

He shrugged. "There is always one packed in the ATV."

"I didn't mean the blanket. I meant… You did it," she said in a near sob as she threw her arms around Luciano. "You saved our lives."

Luc held her in a crushing hug that made his heart pound all the harder, his face pressed to hers for a long, silent moment as the experience brought memories of his brother's crippling accident to the surface. One near miss with catastrophe was enough in one lifetime. If he'd lost his own life, so be it. But if anything had happened to her under his watch, he never would forgive himself.

They'd cheated death, yet an avalanche of need he couldn't escape raced within him. He wanted to ride the adrenaline rush to its fullest and run his palms over her breasts, skim them down her torso, her trim waist, the inviting curve of her hip.

Need, more powerful than he'd felt in years, pounded hot and heavy in him. He ached to celebrate life and crush his lips to hers. Break down the walls of her resistance and unleash the passion he knew surged within her. He wanted to plunge his hard length into her and ride the storm of passion to its fullest.

More than anything, he wanted to break his vow to keep her at arm's length and make her his. Make them one. And that was the last thing he should do.

"That was too close for comfort," he said, voice hoarse with emotion, his mind muddled with duty and desire.

Caprice swallowed hard, hesitant to pull away from the comfort of his embrace. "God, yes. I've never been so terrified in my life."

He gave a rough laugh and set her back from him, holding her at arm's length, his expression intense. "That is the dangerous allure of extreme sports."

The dangerous allure of the man as well? Without a doubt, she decided.

"It's not for me," she said, meaning both.

His lips pressed into a thin line and put distance between them. "Or me."

"The trail is blocked, isn't it?" she asked, knowing the answer before he nodded.

"It will take days to move the ice and rubble."

"But we can get back to the village," she pressed.

"Not today," he said and pointed to the dark clouds roiling over the mountains. "Let's get out of here."

Darkness and perhaps a storm would descend on them soon. They could be stuck here at a remote *rifugio* for tonight. Maybe another day before the track could be cleared. Maybe more. And for once she had left her netbook and papers in her portfolio in her room.

She had nothing to occupy her time except the company of her host, and nobody to blame for being here except herself. She'd insisted on coming up here today because she'd been intent on getting this job done quickly. Her obstinacy had nearly cost them their lives.

They reached another shelf that was far smaller than the other one. "Welcome to my refuge from the world," he shouted.

Her gaze landed on a red-roofed stone building perched on a rocky ledge she estimated was the length of a football field from them. "Finally," she said, teeth chattering.

"Are you all right?" he asked, wrenching around to look at her, brows drawn, eyes dark.

She shook her head. "I'm cold."

"We'll be there soon. Can you hang on a while longer?"

She nodded and slid her arms around his lean waist, pressing close to his body and welcome heat, not caring if he liked it or not. He sighed. Or was it a groan?

Moments that seemed like hours passed before he parked the ATV on the cliff side of the building next to a small stone wall that snaked along the edge of the slope. He vaulted off and helped her dismount, then wrapped an arm around her shoulders and guided her through the gate.

It swung open soundlessly and she preceded him through it onto a paved stone walkway that led to a large wooden deck. Only one door was visible on the side and she headed toward the heavy wooden panel, her wet shoes pounding a weary beat on the deck that wrapped around the front V of the *rifugio*.

He unlocked and opened the door for her, his palm to her back as they hurried inside. "I'll start a fire."

"Okay," she said, hugging herself. "Is there a shower?"

"*Si*, in the bedroom down the hall. Can you manage?"

"I think so." But once she was there, her numb fingers couldn't twist the knob.

Without a word, he opened the door wide, then swept her into his arms, slamming the door behind him. "You are chilled to the bone."

She heard a gruff curse in Italian and felt herself pulled into the corner of the wet room.

Blessed warm water pelted her through her clothes as he slammed his back against the wall, still holding her tight in his arms. She gasped a breath and flung her head back, her fingers clasped behind his neck, glorying in the hot water washing away the grime and cold and fear from her.

He shifted and the hot spray plastered her hair to her head. She turned her head from the force, watching the streaks of brown mire from them both rush across the white tile floor toward the drain.

If only bad memories could be erased that easily.

Her face lifted to the hot spray, the jets washing over her body just like they had done seven years ago as she'd tried to scrub the taint of her attacker's seed and smell from her body. She hadn't thought it important to wash that beast from her soul as well.

She and Luciano had just escaped death. He'd done it at least once before, but this was her first close call. In all the years she'd skied in competition and for fun, she'd never experienced anything that threatened physical devastation or worse. Yet for the past couple of years she'd treated those who had. Dealt with men and women who'd lost the most basic vital functions of mobility.

All of these years she'd thought she understood how her patients must feel because she'd experienced her own demoralizing fear. She'd lost something precious, something she would never have back again. This time, she could have lost more—her life or Luciano's.

Yet she had buried a vital part of her seven years ago.

Rape was death, whether bodily or mentally. It was the last rites of one's innocence. The total stripping of will, power and control. That violation victimized and punished, leaving scars that ran soul deep for years, that haunted the survivor long into the nights to come. It remained the stain that couldn't be washed away, couldn't be removed, couldn't be forgotten.

It victimized, sentencing the wronged to a living hell. It was the prisoners' brand only invisible to the eye, but still she'd hidden the truth from the world out of fear and shame. And just like a devastating accident that sentenced the victims to wheelchairs for life, her rape had left her scarred emotionally.

She had tried then to scrub that stain from her body, but it remained. The mark she couldn't wash away, couldn't forget. It had clung to her for years, just like her sopping clothes did now.

Dirt was dirt and she'd wallowed in that particular filth long enough. She pulled at her T-shirt, at his, desperate to be free of constrictions, of phobias, of pain.

This was her call. Her choice. A beautiful, haunted man held her in his arms. Wanting her on a purely carnal level, judging by the strong hands that held her so tightly, by the hard, rigid length of his anatomy that prodded her hip through her sopping jeans.

She wanted to be rid of them. Wanted to feel the man naked and willing.

For seven years she'd pulled into a shell, refusing to date, refusing even to go out with the girls. She was sick and tired of hiding, of jumping at shadows. She wanted to confront life again. Wanted to be intimate with a man because it was her choice.

All she had to do was reach for what she wanted most. Right now.

She turned in his embrace and wiggled her legs free, slithering down his long legs like a serpent. "What if I said I'd changed my mind?" she said, straddling the edge of flippant.

"About?"

"Sex. Us. Now."

He pulled back, water pouring over his head and streaming down his face as his eyes searched, assessed. "That's the shock of surviving danger talking."

"You don't feel it, too?" she asked, voice hoarse. "God, I feel it," she said, breathless. "But what difference does that make? I want you. Need you now. What more can I say?"

"Nothing. In the end you will expect more than that. An affair, commitment."

She shook her head. "Not anymore. No ties. No promises."

His eyes narrowed, and his hopes and desires soared. "You want my financial backing *and* sex?"

"Yes. We are bound together by a contract, there's no changing that. But when the job is finished, so are we."

"Of course," he replied, his eyes dark and unreadable.

Then his beautiful lips curled in a wolfish smile and he pulled her into his arms, his mouth brushing hers once, twice, before settling in for a lengthy melding of lips and tongue that poured live coals on her desire. The passion burning in his eyes melted her heart, and the heat curling off his body threatened to set hers on fire with raw need.

She moved against him with feline grace, her hands boldly stroking his broad shoulders, the long line of his spine and lean hips, before her fingers splayed over his firm buttocks. He jerked, his erection sliding between her thighs and gracing her core through her clothes. A moan tore from her as the friction of wet bodies moving together stoked the ache pulsing low in her belly.

God, how she wanted this man. Wanted to experience uninhibited sex with him. Wanted this moment to blot out the ugly memory that haunted her deep into the night.

This was her choice. No promises. No regrets. No shame.

The only way to escape the demons in her past was to plunge headlong into the future because she wanted this. She deserved it. She would take it.

CHAPTER FIVE

Luc HADN'T FELT this exhilarated, this alive in years, this impassioned to make love to a woman. And not just any woman.

He wanted Caprice. Wanted her without strings attached. Wanted her now without a thought to tomorrow.

In the course of a few hours she'd changed from businesswoman to an enchanting vixen hungry for sex, nothing more. All the passion she'd infused into her program now fueled her intent to satisfy her needs.

It was sexy as hell. Liberating.

How the hell could he turn his back on that proposition?

He couldn't. He would be the man who satisfied her needs as well as his own.

Without ceremony, he grasped her slender shoulders and levered her away from him, peeling off her wet clothes to reveal a toned body rosy with passion. "You are beautiful. Perfect."

She blinked, lips soft and dewy. Inviting lips. Lips that could pleasure a man, and God knew he selfishly wanted that from her now.

His body pressed her against the tiles, his palms slapping the cool marble while hot water pounded his head and shoulders and streamed over them creating an erotic steam bath of writhing bodies, dueling tongues and sizzling need.

Sweet and spicy. Hot. She was more provocative than any woman he'd kissed, enflaming his desire more than before, nudging deeper feelings in him that had screwed up his mind and his life once before. He shoved those dark thoughts of Isabella away and focused on Caprice, taking everything she would give him before he turned the tables on her and made her whimper and beg for more.

He removed his clothes and circled her slender shoulders in his arms, pulling her closer, tucking her against his rock-hard erection. Her gasp was proof she knew what would come next. That she was ready for his possession.

"Now," he ground out as his erection probed between her legs, desperate to be inside her.

She shifted and his penis grazed her belly, away from the core he ached to explore. He sucked in a sharp breath, his blood fizzing with passion. Was she evading him?

The thought of seducing her quickly shorted and sparked as her hot lips pressed a trail down his chest and her fingernails raked over the taut abdomen, enflaming a blaze of passion that defied the water streaming over them.

"So good," she murmured against his belly, sliding lower.

"Bella," he breathed.

His hands tangled in her wet hair as her sensual fingers stroked him and her hungry mouth ravished and licked and sucked his entire hard length until he was certain he could hold back no longer. He tossed his head back and welcomed the punishing pings of cooler water on his shoulders and face, struggling to hold back his release that threatened to erupt any second, wanting this sensual torture to go on and on. It would be easier to hold the sea in his palms.

"Caprice," he shouted, surrendering to the sweet sensual torture he'd hungered for, barely able to think beyond savoring the exquisite pleasure of her mouth settling over his engorged tip.

Her lips pressed a hot wet trail upward, her knowing hands gliding up his torso in a sultry caress that sparked embers to his semi-sated desire. He wouldn't have guessed this depth of sensuality from her, yet why not?

She was passionate in her work, passionate in her sensuality.

Yes, she was using him for pleasure as much as he was using her, but she had been upfront with him from the start. She'd made clear what she wanted going into their contract as well as the changes she wanted in their arrangement now.

Her professional mind was brilliant, sharp, open. Sex with her would be incredible, addictive.

They could do this, have an affair and walk away without regret or reservations.

He flicked off the shower that had grown cool and sucked in great drafts of air, his body quivering with pleasure from that one taste that left him hungry for more. Since his divorce, he'd had women with little conscious thought, feeling nothing but carnal satisfaction when a fling was over because that's all he'd wanted from them. He would feel the same when his "contract" with Caprice ended.

Theirs was the perfect situation. She was the saving grace for his brother, and for his own choking guilt. He was the means to an end for her. Rich means to finance her new venture. Something she wanted so badly that she'd agreed to share her intuitive knowledge, and now her bed with him. She'd been honest about it. And he would take great satisfaction in making it as pleasurable for them both in work *and* in play.

His palms skimmed down her spine, which was tight

with muscle and tension. His ego swelled as she moaned and pressed closer. Needy. Trusting. Giving.

His lips captured hers and he drank the passion still wet on her lips, a drugging sensual brew that tossed hot embers on the emotions banked in his heart and soul. Whatever her reasons for pleasuring him first were, they were hers. He was grateful for the amazing rush, and he would repay the favor. In fact he looked forward it.

"I am the reflection of you at this moment," he said, sliding his arm around her slender shoulders, tucking her close and relishing the feel of her in his arms.

Her hushed laugh was bells on the wind, soft and fleeting. "I don't believe it."

He smoothed her wet hair back and cupped her face in his palms, staring into eyes that never stayed locked with his for long, as if hiding something and afraid he'd discover her secrets. Like his wife?

"Why do you doubt me?" he asked, pushing thoughts of Isabella away, not wanting her dark memory to shadow this pleasure he felt now.

"You're a man, operating on a different level than women. You take what you want when you want it without reservations or regrets."

"As you just did with me."

Her cheeks turned pink, an odd reaction for a woman who'd just taken the initiative to indulge in fellatio. But then Caprice was unlike any woman he'd ever known.

Her chin came up and her palm skimmed down his bare belly, stopping inches from where he throbbed for her touch. "I took what I wanted without regrets."

"And now it is my turn, *bella*," he said.

"What if I've had enough?" she asked.

He grabbed a soft bath sheet and wrapped it around her beautifully naked body, drawing her flush against him.

Then he slipped his leg between hers and caught the quiver of need that shot through her. "You haven't."

A provocative look and a promising smile was all it took to enflame his desire to a fever pitch again. It had been a long time since he'd taken this much time and pleasure with a woman, despite what the tabloids boasted. His choice, just as this was his decision to make now. He wanted more from her. He'd have it.

She'd invaded his sanctuary. He'd never allowed another woman to do that and had sworn on the drive up that he wouldn't tolerate it happening again.

This was a onetime shot. It was nothing beyond the duration of their contract.

His lips adored her closed eyelids, teased the curve of her ears and cooled cheeks, still charmingly rosy, before capturing her sweet lips in a long, drugging kiss that left his head spinning. His hunger for her consumed him, but he took care lowering her to the carpeted floor and following her down, lounging beside her when his body demanded he plunge into her hot depths and find his satiation now.

His palm took a meandering route up her torso to full creamy breasts bearing hard nipples with dark rose areolae that puckered from the change of temperature from hot shower to marginally cooler chamber. He lowered his head to nuzzle and kiss and adore the soft flesh under both breasts in turn, lifting them closer with cupped palms to the torment of his tongue and mouth.

Her lithe body twisted and arched; the soft sounds she was making were invitations to take her right now.

And he would, laying a wet trail of kisses down her tight torso and flat belly, his tongue circling her navel once, twice, before settling down at the juncture of her thighs.

A skim of his fingers over her bare folds told him she was still wet and ready. And his!

"Luciano!"

"Bella, amore mio."

He dipped his head to taste her lightly, then treated her to a deep, sensual kiss. Her back arched off the floor, fingernails digging into his shoulders, a high keen coming from her softly parted lips. A guttural moan of satisfaction escaped him as he kissed her, stroked her, probed her depths to the limits, his own body tight and throbbing with the need to release.

Again he was struck by the rightness of being with her. Had he ever felt this intense before? Had it ever felt this perfect?

And once again his mind was blank of everything except the woman in his arms. He needed her. Needed to get his fill of her so he would be free of her memory.

He slid his palms under her soft bottom and held her to him, loving her deeply, her fingers grasping his shoulders, his hair, only fueling his rising passion to a crashing crescendo. She arched again, her body trembling with spasm after spasm. Her climax peaked not one second too late before his own need threatened to explode.

In one smooth push, he entered her, sliding up over her body, satisfied as her legs parted wide to welcome him home. And that was just what it felt like as he thrust into her again and again, struggling to hold back his release until she shattered into another climax. He held her tight and let go, his body violently jerking as he reached for his own summit.

Drained, sated, he collapsed on her, his head resting on her shoulder, numb with pleasure. A sense of completeness pulsed around them.

This was right. Perfect.

No! She was right. Perfect. He'd needed this. Needed her at this moment.

That was all. He could still walk away from her at any time without regrets.

Caprice ran her palms up his damp back, her fingers skimming the hard muscles that were now lax and felt boneless herself. Complete. She hadn't expected this afterglow to hum through her softly, lulling her more deeply into relaxation like she'd known before.

"That was amazing," she whispered against his shoulder.

He shifted enough to look down on her, hand gliding down her side, igniting that slow burn of desire all over again. "You are amazing."

She laughed at his compliment, not believing it for a moment.

"What's wrong?" he asked.

"Nobody has ever told me that before."

"Then your previous lovers were all fools."

She sobered at that. "I've only had sex once before," she said, and wanted to bite her tongue off for admitting that much.

He shifted to look at her, and she averted her eyes, preferring to stare at the dark whorls of hair on his muscled chest. "Once?"

She nodded, not daring to look up.

"Not a memorable experience?"

"Not one I care to bring to mind," she said, hating that memories of that night threatened to rush back to life, to taint the pleasure she'd just experienced.

She shook her head, willing the dark past to retreat into the recesses of her mind. But the voices remained, a low nagging whisper of pleas and cries and threats, a living reminder of that night, that man's total domination over her, and the ugly violation she'd lived with for years.

A woman never forgot being raped. She'd become an expert at keeping people at arm's length until Luciano came back into her life.

He grasped her chin and forced her to face him, blue eyes intent on hers. "You will tell me someday, yes?"

That was the last thing she would do, now or ever. But admitting that would only prompt him to pester her for details she never wanted to reveal.

"Someday," she lied.

She'd told no one she'd been raped by Luciano's friend, afraid to challenge the threat her attacker had issued, wanting the whole thing buried. Forgotten. She intended to keep it that way.

And she had to believe that man had done the same. She'd certainly never heard any rumors connecting them, and Luciano seemed ignorant of the entire thing. Of all people, she would think he would have known and was so glad he didn't.

For her, it would always be the black day in her life, over and done with but she would never forget. After seven years, nothing would be served by telling anyone, especially Luciano. She'd moved on. Hopefully she would never cross paths with that horrible man again.

"I have given you one good memory, but that isn't enough, *bella*." He dropped a kiss on her forehead, her cheeks, his lips hovering over hers. "Let's make more for both of us."

"Yes," she breathed before his lips captured hers in a long, lazy kiss that sparked fire in the desire banked inside her, making her feel wanted, needed.

"Yes," she whispered again between breaths, locking the door on the past and opening wide the portal to the present. She welcomed Luciano into her arms, her heart, as they plunged into the warm surf of passion, wanting to remember it when the darkness and fears intruded.

He was a drug in her veins and her blood fizzed, her control spiraling downward into a tide pool of passion. For one split second she nearly pulled back into her protective shell. But another searing kiss, coupled with the hot possessive glide of his hands up and down her back, banished the urge, making her want more of his touch, his kiss, his possession.

Her hands sought and found the hard, pulsing length of him. He groaned, rocking into her palm, as if begging her fingers to explore him. She did, stroking the silk-over-steel erection that grew in her palm. Her heartbeat quickened, the core of her wet and throbbing with want.

Her other hand slid down his thigh, the muscles there hard and powerful to a point. And then…she stilled, frowning as her fingers recognized the change in skin and the uneven shape. A scar, and a very deep one, she suspected.

"Enough playing," he said, dragging her exploring hand to his chest.

His fingers found her core, stroking, teasing, and the questions that had ballooned to her mind popped. Each stroke strummed a lover's song that whispered around them like silken ribbons, the melody intoxicating to her senses.

She'd dreamed of being loved like this for years, not believing it could ever come true. That sex with a man could only be better if she imagined it.

Now she knew that wasn't true. Now that Luciano was literally in the palm of her hands, she would savor this forever. Her timidity and hard-learned caution diminished as desire and awareness of her own sensuality increased.

There was power in sex. Power in her own needs. Power in satisfying his as well.

She would deal with the consequences of embarking on an affair tomorrow, or the next day, or whenever they returned to the real world. For now she just wanted to savor the pleasure.

Luc lay on his back, staring at the ceiling. The lull of her even breathing and relaxed body tempted him to sleep as well. Yet old demons chose now to haunt him and remind him how close he'd come again to letting tender emotions blind him.

He was right there on the edge, enjoying this special moment with Caprice, wanting to believe she was nearly innocent. But how could he? Was it possible for a vibrant, passionate woman to have had experienced sex once yet satisfy a man of his experience?

His heart said yes but his cynical mind warned something was off, that she was not being straight with him.

He'd learned to distrust women from the best.

Isabella had been a very convincing liar. She'd said all the right words and done all the right things. His charming, deceitful wife had had great fun with the lofty position marriage to him had afforded her and had enjoyed spending his money on her every whim.

She'd relished using him.

Tension tightened his muscles and glazed his heart in ice, for he'd never denied her anything.

Isabella had been the supreme actress, sleeping in his bed and his arms every night. Professing her love.

A damned lie. She'd sneaked away during the day to be with her lover.

The hell of it was he hadn't known, hadn't suspected. Perhaps he never would have if he hadn't spontaneously decided to fly to London and surprise her there during one of her solo shopping trips.

That was the end of his marriage. Divorce was the expected outcome, and she hadn't fought it, seeking only a fat settlement.

Looking back on it now, he wondered if he should have gone through his life loving her, loving any children produced of their marriage. If he could have found contentment, she would be alive today. But he'd sent her away. Shamed. Scorned.

And she'd died in a horrible auto accident.

Guilt was a horrible thing to bear. His wife's death. His brother's crippling accident. Both could be laid at his door.

Those events had changed him. Hardened him.

Right now they were tainting a good moment in his life with Caprice that he wanted to preserve in memory. Yet how could he when he suspected she was lying to him about something in her past?

It would be impossible until he got to the truth.

That would come. He would uncover her secrets before he made another costly mistake with a woman.

Caprice wasn't sure who fell asleep first, or who awakened first. One moment she was sated and warm lying in his arms on the floor. The next he was gently tipping her face to his and staring at her with eyes that always saw too much.

"Are you okay?" he asked, his voice rough.

"Yes. Fine." Better than she thought she'd be, and that alone told her she'd made the right decision.

"Why didn't you tell me you had only had one lover before me?"

Because she hadn't had a lover. Her attacker didn't deserve that title.

"What difference does it make?" she asked.

He heaved a sigh. "None, I guess. I just thought…you'd had more experience. Hell, I thought you'd had experience when I met you at the World Cup."

"I admit I was naive but fearless." To her own peril.

"I have thought long and hard about how poorly I treated you in the past," he bit out, as if hating to admit that much.

"It's okay. I was too young to understand that relationships were all a game to you." Too young to realize that some men were only out to use and abuse.

She reached up to cup his jaw, desperate to connect with the man who'd just pleasured her beyond belief. Had granite ever felt this hard? She chanced a peek at him. Had blue eyes ever looked so icy cold?

He grasped her hand and pulled it away, and she felt the distancing yawn between them, felt the old rejection nip at her nerves. "I did you a favor, *bella*."

"It didn't feel like it at the time." She rolled away and got to her feet, wrapping the towel around her naked body, breaking the physical contact, but still plagued with a jumble of good and bad memories.

"I was in the wake of a bitter divorce. You knew that."

She nodded. "I heard rumors surrounding the end of your marriage and none of it put you in a good light. Is it true you threatened divorce unless your wife got a paternity test?"

He got to his feet, unabashedly naked. "Yes, which she refused to do. If you knew that, then why didn't you ask me if it was true?"

"I didn't believe you would do such a thing to your family." Even now she had trouble accepting his matter-of-fact confession.

"You'd heard the truth and yet you flirted with me." He shook his head. "My God, you were naive."

"I call it trusting and loyal," she added. And she still was in many respects.

"Yes, you have always been that way to me," he said, eyes drilling into her so intimately she felt as if he were touching her still. "But that is not why I wanted you now."

"You've made it clear from the start that you simply wanted rights to my therapy program," she said. "I don't have a problem with that or what just happened between us."

She knew any relationship with him would simply be carnal lust. No emotional ties. No commitments. No promises.

His women were conveniences. Well paid, if the rumors were true. And well loved, if only physically. Now she was one of them.

"Good." He stalked to the door and paused to look back at her. "You should be able to find suitable clothes in the closet. When you're dressed, meet me in the great room."

Then he was gone, not giving her the option to agree or balk. But then why would she?

She'd gotten what she asked for. No more. It was time to view this amazing design that may, or may not, be suitable for the therapy pod. Then she would get back to the lodge and reality.

Solitude. That's what she needed to put all of this back into perspective, and soon.

Fifteen minutes later she found jeans and jerseys, still bearing tags, hanging in the closet. Considering she had nothing to wear, and refusing to belabor the point of wearing something intended for another woman, she rid them of the tags and dressed, then finished towel-drying her hair.

She was clean and incredibly charged with energy, considering the day's events, when she walked into the great room. And stopped.

The amazing expanse of glass on either side of the massive stone fireplace, complete with roaring fire, made it feel as if they were suspended over a fathomless gorge, as if she were hanging on to this primitive ledge. She couldn't image a more perfect view.

"I've never quite seen anything like this," she said, near breathless.

"Is that good or bad?" he asked, the warmth of his body against hers telling her he was far too near again.

"Good. Has this place been in your family for long?"

Again, the crooked smile that made her skin tingle and her stomach tighten. "No. I acquired it after my first World Cup win with intention of restoring it to a quality *rifugio*."

"But you didn't," she guessed.

He shook his head, his smile disappearing like the clouds that suddenly shrouded the jagged peaks in the distance. "Because of the disrepair here, it took undue time restoring it. So long, in fact, that I'd begun to long for a secret place to get away from the world. But the wait was worth it."

She took it all in, understanding his need for a retreat and finding this very nice, very relaxing and cozy. "Is this the design that you thought I would love?"

"No, that is upstairs. After you," he said, making a sweeping motion toward the multiple landings of the long staircase that separated the great room from the galley area, suddenly treating her as a guest.

The low risers between the trio of landings said more about his need for rest than any explanation could convey. Each landing provided a place to pause with an arresting vista that differed from the one before it. They were a reminder of the majestic mountains and challenging runs that would call to any accomplished skier.

Yet Luciano hadn't gone back. This was the retreat he'd

designed for himself. Where he could hide and heal his broken body. But what about his troubled soul? she wondered.

That question troubled her as she reached the top level. It took her a moment to scan the massive space. *Peaceful* was the only word that came to mind. The furnishings were dressed in variant blues and browns and whites, colors that melded in with artistic murals and the living landscape vista just beyond the two walls of glass, which opened naturally onto the vast sky and rugged mountain range.

"This is it," he said, pride and something indefinable resonating in his voice.

He didn't have to tell her this was his bedroom. She knew it the second she walked in.

The entire space felt as vast as the rugged range, dominated by a bed that screamed pleasure. And she knew that was exactly what she would find there.

She looked away from it, body burning and tingling anew. What had happened to the instinctual warning that heartache would be the end result of an affair? Was the promised pleasure worth the pain that would come?

"This is beyond unique," she said, focusing on the design again instead of the arresting man who threatened to dominate her thoughts, who made her trust him, want him. "The architectural and interior design make the entire space seem as if I am standing on the mountain."

"Yes." He remained by the window, his back to her now. "This place helped heal me."

"After the accident?"

He nodded. "My ex-wife's death as well. Can you understand that?"

"Yes, I think so. You loved her. Grieved her death."

He scrubbed a hand along his nape and sighed. "It is

true. Many of my friends could not understand why I cared, why I shut myself away after her death."

"Who asked for the divorce?"

"I did." He braced an arm on the window and stared out at the vista. "Does that surprise you?"

She wouldn't lie. "In a way."

He faced her then, back to the window and arms locked over his chest, a wall keeping anyone from getting too close. "I found her in bed, in the arms of another man. It was an ugly confrontation with passions and tempers running high. Finally she admitted that he was her lover and their affair had been going on long before our marriage."

She pressed her fingertips to her mouth, unable to imagine how awful it would be to catch your loved one cheating. "You must have been heartbroken."

"Yes, but I was furious over her betrayal," he said, his voice dark.

"If she had a lover she refused to leave, why did she marry you?"

"Marriage afforded her a lavish allowance, the bulk of which ended up funneled to him, I suspect." He drummed his fingers on the glass panel, his expression remote. "They were expecting a child."

She cringed at the added pain Luciano went through. "So you divorced her."

"As quickly and quietly as possible."

She shook her head, stunned that the ugly rumors she'd heard about Isabella Duchelini were true. Betrayal like Luciano had received at his wife's hand cut to the heart and drew blood that stained a soul.

In many ways he was starting over, but only partially.

"Why didn't you return to skiing?" she asked.

His shoulders shifted into such a tight line she was surprised she didn't hear the twang of muscles and tendons snap and break. "I had my reasons." He faced her, all warmth gone from his features, making it clear he wasn't going to share those reasons with her, so she forced herself to change the subject. "You paid more attention to tactile detail, which in turn reflected the mood that resonated with you."

"Good, you see it, too," he said, and she nodded. "I didn't realize how very much I needed a retreat until the accident."

She certainly understood the desperate need to escape a horrible incident. Her refuge had been her lodge and a redirection of her life. Taking control again, if only in baby steps.

In time, the personal attack she'd suffered receded to the back of her mind. It was rarely recalled, yet the pain and shame were never forgotten.

No, she didn't have to ask how much his loss and his terrible accident pained him emotionally and physically. One look at his drawn features proved he suffered deeply on both levels.

"I wish I would have been able to help you then," she said, hesitating before laying her hand atop his.

But on what level could she have helped? Emotionally? Maybe. Physically? Not likely considering what she'd endured.

She would like to think she could have put her own feelings aside, but in all honesty she wasn't sure. It had taken her years to recover to this stage. And besides, the point was moot as that was the time she'd delved deeper into her studies, putting her degree first in her life and taking that vow to go it alone.

He brushed off her hand and stormed to the window. "I couldn't think beyond my own need to be alone. Secluded." He shook his head. "I don't expect you to understand."

"But I do," she said, batting at the unwelcome tears stinging her eyes, debating if she should tell him what had happened that night he'd left her.

Why? What good would it serve? None.

"I have lived with shame and fear and the desperate need to escape the world my mother adored," she said instead.

He hung his head, jaw clenched. "I didn't know that pained you so much, but then I was too wrapped up in my own problems and needs. What else can I say to convince you that I am truly sorry for my past behavior?"

"Nothing. Explanations aren't necessary." *For either of them.* She shook her head, shelving that dark past where it belonged. "Did you hire me because you regretted how you treated me in the past?"

"No. I told you it was because you are the best at what you do and I meant it. The past had nothing to do with it." He grasped her hand and she could have sworn she saw sparks fly from the contact. God knew she felt the burn to the depths of her soul. "What can I do to ease your mind, Caprice? Tell me."

"You're doing it." She forced a smile, grateful she could still feel the trembles deep inside her.

"Good." He rubbed his hands together and smiled, a far more relaxed expression than she thought him capable of. "Am I right then? Do you like this and feel it is the perfect design for the adaptive program?"

She turned in a slow circle, absorbing the pulse of this amazing space, liking it. No, she loved it. Felt the energy flowing here. "You're right. It's amazing—this design makes me feel strong and capable of doing anything."

"It is the inspiration I covet." He took a deep breath and blew it out. "I'm loath to share it, but because it will benefit others, I give it to you."

For a long moment she studied his solemn expression, judging if he was sincere. If relinquishing his private design somehow took the beauty and serenity from him.

"I accept this with pride and honor and thanks." She entwined her fingers and drank in this sense of calmness and power again, not ever wanting to lose that. "I'm anxious to get going on this. Will we be able to leave tomorrow?"

He barked a laugh. "If we're lucky."

She sobered. "Are you kidding?"

"It could take days to clear the destruction left by the avalanche."

She nodded, exuberance slouching a bit. "You're sure?"

"Yes. It has happened before." He crossed to her and clasped her shoulders, his blue eyes turning seductively smoky. "For now, we wait for word when the road is cleared."

"And do what?" she asked.

His wolfish smile was answer enough.

Caprice opened her eyes slowly, every muscle in her body deliciously relaxed. It was too dark to guess the time, but at some point he'd taken her to bed. And they'd never left it.

She smiled and stretched, feeling a bit wicked being naked beneath the silk sheet with his scent on her, around her, the heat of him so near she remained comfortably warm. "Are you asleep?"

"No," he said gruffly in a sleep-roughened voice. "I'm too hungry. Are you?"

Her stomach answered in a low rumble and they both laughed. "Definitely. And this time for something besides sex."

"Can you cook?"

"Sure. I help out in my kitchen at the lodge all the time," she said, a bit confused. "Why do you ask?"

"While we were sleeping, I received a text from my housekeeper. She tried to bring the monthly supplies to the *rifugio*, and discovered the trail blocked, so they went back to la Duchi Royal."

"So someone knows we're up here?"

"That was never an issue. Anyway, they are safe in the village and wanted to make sure we'd escaped the avalanche." He pulled her from the bed and draped his shirt around her shoulders, his own long, lean body beautifully naked and aroused in the arrows of moonlight that targeted him. "Come on. Let's raid the kitchen."

She shrugged her arms into his shirt and rolled the sleeves up to her wrists, enjoying the glimpse of him thrusting long, strong legs into jeans that rode decadently low on his hips. "The ATV is low on petrol and my housekeeper assured me there was none to be found here, so seeking a route higher up is out of the question."

"We can't get down the mountain and nobody can get up it. And supplies here are obviously limited," she said, the isolation of being here with him finally sinking in. "How long will it take before the trail is cleared?"

"Typically the crews have the route reopened in less than a week," he said, his frown saying otherwise. "But this was an exceptionally wicked avalanche. It could take longer."

"I suppose attempting to descend the mountain on skis is out of the question?"

"That would be too dangerous to attempt."

Was she really hearing this from the man who thrived to test the limits on the slopes? "But—"

"We'll wait for the trail to be cleared," he cut in, his brow pulled into a dark scowl that dared her to argue.

Not that she would.

Taking an off-piste route around the avalanche was too

risky to attempt for anyone who wasn't a top skier. Her skills were higher than most, but nothing to compare to him. Or at least to the skier he'd been. Now? If he couldn't attempt the run with full confidence, then they were right in staying here until the trail was safe to travel.

"Okay," she said, content to follow him down the wide hallway until she noticed that he favored his right leg. The same limb where her fingers had skimmed a ridge of skin before he'd pulled her hand away. "Your right side took the brunt of the injury when you fell that day on the Hahnenkamm. That's why you don't ski."

He came to a dead stop and looked back at her, eyes glacial hard again. "I wondered how long it would take you to notice."

"It's not that obvious," she said, and when he raised a questioning eyebrow, she shrugged. "I'm trained to catch things the average person wouldn't see."

"As I said before, you are extremely astute. But you're wrong about one thing. My injuries are not why I quit skiing." He continued down the hall without explaining more, leaving her to wonder the real reason.

She entered a large kitchen that boasted an array of copper pots and skillets, their shiny surfaces gleaming from the sun streaming through the bank of windows. "But your abilities were diminished by the accident?"

He nodded. "My injuries were severe. As soon as I was able, I began rebuilding muscle tone. But the right side didn't fully return, leaving me with one-sided strength. I can ski. Do pretty much anything I want," he said, his gaze skimming over her body once, twice, as if reminding her of the pleasure they'd just shared, before settling on her eyes again. "But I would be a fool to attempt competition again."

"You could ski for pleasure," she said.

"I skied to win. Now it's over." He spread his arms and turned in the center of the large kitchen. "Let's see how good you are at concocting a meal out of thin provisions."

And just like that, he had swiftly changed topic again. Normally she'd never have given up this easily with a client, but then, as he'd reminded her, he wasn't her patient.

"Your chef has excellent taste in cookware."

He laughed as he rummaged through a massive twin-door refrigerator that looked rather stark. "The cookware is my preference."

"Seriously? You cook?" she asked, and bit back adding, *more than a box meal.*

"Of course I can. I love good food and have always known how most can be best prepared," he said, kissing the pinched tips of his forefinger and thumb in such an exaggerated, theatrical way she laughed, thoroughly enjoying this freedom with a man. "It seemed logical that I learned how to prepare these dishes as well. One lesson from a chef in Tuscany and I was hooked on cooking."

She shook her head and smiled, liking this playful, relaxed side of Luciano. Liking it a bit too much perhaps. But she'd come this far. She might as well enjoy this companionship with a man while it lasted.

"I had no idea you possessed such hidden talents," she teased.

He laughed, a rich contralto that hummed within her. "Are you hungry, *bella*?"

"Ravenous." She moved to him and stroked a hand down his chest, feeling far bolder than she ever had with a man.

"Hmm, would you like Italian?"

She trailed a fingernail down his breastbone and had the satisfaction of hearing him draw a sharp breath, his blue eyes darkening to near black. "Are we talking food or the man?"

"Both." He bent close, capturing her lips for a kiss that was far too brief. "What would the lady like first?"

Her stomach chose that moment to release a low growl. Or had that sound bubbled from her throat?

"I get my choice between a fantastic meal or you?"

"But of course. It is always your choice."

"Then I choose you," she said against his lips.

He drew her flush against his length, his mouth teasing the corners of her mouth, her nose, her eyes before melding over her, lips, tongue flicking her teeth, tasting and taunting. His hands explored her shoulders, his palms smooth, the fingers strong as they trailed down her back, over her hips before cupping her bottom and sweeping her up in his arms. Any protest she made, not that she could utter more than a gasp, was stopped by the slow, erotic thrust of his tongue against her own.

"Bella, mio amore," he said, flicking the buttons open on the shirt to free her breasts, his palm cupping one and brushing a thumb over the nipple before his mouth captured it, nuzzling and drawing it in deeply, doing the same to its twin in turn.

Fire raged through her blood, a sensual inferno that could only be put out by his possession. She dug her fingernails into his back, lost to desire, not caring how or where he took her as long as it was now.

"Love me," she husked against his head, threading her fingers through the dampening strands of his hair and pressing closer to his ravishing mouth, feeling his blood pulsing in his temples and the tension vibrating in his arms.

"With pleasure," he husked out, taking her down on the counter, his weight barely suspended above her, his hot, hard erection probing her swollen flesh that was damp with desire for him again.

This time there was no hesitation, no sense of awkwardness alive in her. The trust she'd once had returned, along with the longing she'd held close for him. But that longing had come alive at his touch, and she reveled in being wanton in his arms, consumed by the promise of pleasure that blazed in his blue eyes, a promise she'd tasted once and hungered for again.

He rocked forward above her and she lifted her hips to meet his downward thrust. She gasped as they smoothly became one. He released a grunt of pure masculine satisfaction and held her tightly, still and hard within her, hearts thundering from the storm raging within them.

In that moment, suspended in passion, she thought she could stay like this forever and yet knew she could barely take another moment of this sensual torment, tasted but far from sated. And then, thankfully, artfully, erotically he moved, slowly pulling back from her core before thrusting into her so hard and deeply she saw stars flickering behind her closed eyes. Heaven. She was but a breath from it and it was far more glorious than she'd dreamed it could be.

"Look at me," he ordered. "Look at me when you climax, *bella*."

She did, blinking until her eyes focused. Her breath caught in her throat as his gaze bore into her, holding her tighter than any bond could.

"I could drown in your eyes," she said.

"If you did," he gasped as he moved inside her with deliciously torturing thrusts, "I would follow you down and bring you back to me."

Tears stung her eyes and she swallowed hard, engulfed in passion, emotion, confusion. He couldn't mean that.

"Why?" she asked on a caught breath, staring into his

eyes dark with passion, fingernails digging into his powerful upper arms.

"For this." He grasped her hips and pushed hard into her, features strained, cords in his neck standing like ropes.

She arched her back, rubbing her hot body against his scorching one, muscles clenched in her core, encasing his erection. A shout, or was it a scream, tore through the air. She didn't know. Didn't care. Only this moment mattered with their bodies joined. His hot seed spilled inside her, his erection rubbing the sensitive nub that he'd brought to life.

A rainbow of light flickered behind her eyes and her breath caught, her senses soaring into the stratosphere. Time had no meaning as she gloried in the sensations.

One last delicious spasm rippled through her and she collapsed, savoring the high of passion. Nothing compared. Not even taking to the air on skis with only the wind beneath her.

His weight came down on her, muscles slowly relaxing, body still burning hot. Both welcome. She needed his warmth. Needed the grounding of slowly returning to the present.

Tension pulled at her, threatening to erode this bliss.

His shoulders and head lifted off her, his brow furrowed, his gaze boring into hers. "What is wrong? Am I too heavy for you?"

"No! I just—" She shook her head and looked away, not wanting to admit the concern this need for him caused her now.

He cupped her chin, forcing her to look at him. "What? Tell me."

"I...working together, if this ends badly..."

"This was a mutual surrender to passion," he said, guessing at her concern, his lips curling into a seductive smile. "Nothing more, nothing less."

Her words in their most basic form. "You're right."

"Don't look for the bad to happen." He took her hand and held it. "Not here, not now."

She nodded, but she didn't trust him, couldn't trust him, any more than she did her ability to control her desires around him. Being lovers for the time she was in Italy was inevitable. She wouldn't argue that point. Nor would she deny him or herself that wondrous pleasure, but she wouldn't play the fool, believing every promise, every sweet lie that tumbled from a lover's lips.

With Luciano she would take what he offered. Savor it. Revel in the pleasure. She would enjoy the present and not worry about the future.

CHAPTER SIX

LUC STOOD ON the deck overlooking the precipice and welcomed the sun beating down on his face, staring out over the vast Alps yet not focusing on anything. His mind was elsewhere, just as it had been the past three days.

It seemed ironic that he'd balked over bringing Caprice to his *rifugio* and now dreaded the thought of leaving here. His reasons were purely selfish.

He'd had the pleasure of having her in his bed surrendering to passion and didn't want it to end. When was the last time he'd spent this much time alone with a woman and enjoyed it?

He shook his head, unable to recall one. Even when he was married, he and Isabella had never spent much more than a day together without it ending in an argument.

But while his compatibility with Caprice was stronger than what he'd had with his wife, he well understood she was using him just the same. The only difference was that he'd known going into it that Caprice was only interested in his money.

He scraped his fingers through his windblown hair and swore. If he was honest with himself, he was more than fond of Caprice. He admired her. Cared deeply for her. Lusted for her.

Though he'd been sure that once he'd tasted her passion

his ardor would cool, his craving for her this morning disproved that theory. She'd quickly become the wildfire in his blood, and sex only fanned the flames. As did thinking about making love with her, he thought sourly, which was happening too frequently.

Their affair was short-term at best. So what if her reasons for being with him were selfish? He could be that way as well, wanting her only for the incredible sex.

That did not have to change when they returned to the lodge, which would be soon. As of an hour ago, the track was cleared and his housekeeper and caretaker had started back to the *rifugio*.

There was no reason for him and Caprice to remain here when their careers and obligations demanded they return to the lodge. Once there, he saw no reason why they couldn't continue their affair for the duration of the contract.

It would simply be convenient. A mutual give and take. They would both get what they wanted without worry over lasting entanglements. Surely she would not object to that.

He whirled on a heel and entered to the bedroom. If they hurried they could be on the road in thirty minutes or less, giving them plenty of time to return to the lodge before dark.

The bed was empty, save the pile of crumpled bedding that streamed from the bed to the floor. "Caprice?"

"I'm here."

He spun around to find her standing in the en suite doorway, eyes wide and sheet clutched to her bosom. The mirror behind her showcased her firm spine and feminine curves of a near-perfect body. Not model perfect. She was "seductive woman" perfect.

"Did you want something?" she asked, clutching the bath sheet tighter, which only emphasized the enticing globes of her bottom.

Her show of modesty made him smile.

"I got a text from my housekeeper. The track is clear."

Her eyes brightened. "We can leave then?"

"As soon as we can."

"Great," she said, moving toward the clothes she'd been wearing off and on for days, though in reality they had been more off of late. "I need to get to work quickly on the project if I'm to have it completed in a month or less."

He crossed to her and took her in his arms, loosely caging her there as he bent for a kiss. Sweet as honey. "The time frame is totally up to you. I am not rushing you."

She planted her palms on his chest and sighed, her gaze pausing at his chin before lifting to meet his eyes. "I know, but I want to finish your contract so I can get busy on Tregore Lodge. There's much to do there."

"You are anxious to return home."

"Of course," she said, chin coming up. "I've never hidden that fact."

"No, you haven't."

She'd stated her priorities up front. How could he argue with that?

"We will leave when you are ready," he said, striding to the door. "I'll wait for you in the great room."

Within an hour, his housekeeper had arrived with supplies and petrol for the ATV and Caprice was ready to leave. Her anxiousness annoyed him, despite the fact he'd expected her to react just as she had. He'd had no doubts she would abide by their contract, but what of their relationship? Was it over in her eyes? Would he be able to seduce her into his bed again?

He would. Somehow, someway.

The drive back to the village was uneventful, save the brief pause he made at the site of the avalanche. Plows had cleared a wide path in the track and had heavy gravel packed on the roadbed. But it wouldn't last the winter.

To his surprise her arms crept around his waist, and she rested her head on his shoulder. "If not for your swift reactions, we would have died."

He nodded, feeling a chill pass through him. "If I'm the cat with nine lives, I had better start using caution as I've expended at least five of them."

"On the slopes?"

"Not all of them."

"Oh?"

He shrugged. "I went through a rather reckless phase in my life."

She sat up, denying him the pleasure of her closeness. "I suppose all boys do that, especially if they are athletes."

And especially if they suffered betrayal and deceit from the one person they loved and trusted. "It's a rite of passage for most, but I cannot blame my exploits on youth."

"Really?" she asked, her small hands resting on his shoulders, reminding him of how tightly she'd held on to him when she'd climaxed. "What spurred your recklessness?"

He sucked in a breath and blew it out, letting the pain of that period in his life knife through him, wanting to remember every single detail so he wouldn't repeat mistakes. "My divorce. It was messy at the end."

Silence echoed in the mountains before she finally broke it. "Want to talk about it?"

"No." Talking about his dead ex-wife with his current lover was the very last thing he ever wished to do. "We need to get moving."

And with that he threw the ATV into gear and sped back down the track, mindful of the woman behind him. Of the lack of contact he received from her now.

She was shelving him away. Her wild romance in the Alps was over for her. She would delve into her work, avoiding him whenever possible.

So would he, but he wasn't done with her yet. No, he'd barely begun. Before the week was out, he would have her in his arms again, willing and wild.

Caprice sat behind Luciano, refusing to grasp the rails for balance instead of the tall, strong man maneuvering the ATV with precision and speed down the rutted trail. Instead of the bracing odor of evergreens and fresh air, she was enveloped by the enticing scent of Luciano.

She supposed it had been inevitable that they fall into each other's arms, finally indulging in the passion that she'd felt toward him for years. For him she understood it was simply having sex.

Fine. She didn't want ties here. Didn't want to lose her heart. This was never supposed to be anything more than a fling. A chance encounter to explore passions. To replace horrible, ugly memories with something beautiful. Something that was her choice.

She had a life and career waiting for her in Colorado. She had aspirations of independence. Of having a peaceful, happy, fulfilled life.

Not once had she thought that she would let Luciano get to her heart again. But she had. Even now it was as if he were pulsing in her blood and stroking her skin. If she closed her eyes she felt him coursing thick and hot through her body, tugging and pushing her over the edge of passion when she least expected it.

He'd left her out of control. Reckless, not with her body but with her heart.

That was where she'd failed before. As an athlete she'd had a margin of upper edge over physical balance. But that training didn't carry over into emotional stability. It didn't shield her heart from the onslaught of emotions she couldn't stop or control.

And that terrified her.

She was comfortable when she was in control. When she was with Luciano, she was horribly off balance. And to think it had only taken him a few days to break down the barriers she'd built around her heart.

For three days and nights she'd made love with him every possible way. Her choice. She'd wanted pleasure from him. Perhaps if she was honest she wanted to revisit the past, to do over what had gone so horribly wrong one cold winter night.

But she hadn't wanted to involve her heart. Hadn't wanted to fall a bit more in love with him as the minutes passed. Love?

Ha! How could she love a man who'd rejected her before? Who only wanted her for sex now? Never mind that she'd told herself she wanted this affair with him for pure pleasure. She'd been the one to seduce him.

That realization left no room for complaints. They were getting what they wanted from each other at the moment. As she'd told him, when the job was over, so was their fling.

Those words reminded her that she was tied to him for the duration of their contract. She would still have him in her bed, his strong arms banding around her while his steely length pulsed inside her, filling her with heat and passion. Banishing the emptiness within her.

But staying here with him meant she wouldn't be free of the crazy nervous upheaval of emotions rioting within her. That wouldn't happen until she left Italy and Luciano. Then she'd be free.

She was strong enough to have an affair and walk away with only battered emotions. She would survive.

She would welcome these memories of Luciano over those that haunted her with his old friend.

That was the promise she made to herself as she lifted her face to the setting sun. When her job here was finished, she would dredge up the courage to walk away with her head held proud, no matter how much a part of her would stay with him forever.

Luciano topped another undulating rise and she spied the village just below. He whipped over one long easy slope and they were there in the thick of it. Shop owners paused to wave as they passed. And up on the high step rose the majestic la Duchi Royal.

She drank it all in and reveled in the sensory buzz that hummed like a swarm of happy bees. Here she could get back to work instead of chasing hot pursuits with Luciano. She would distance herself from him during the day. If timing permitted, she would spend time with him at night.

If not? So be it. She couldn't think any other way and remain sane.

Once she focused her thoughts on installing her program in Luciano's new facility, this hurt needling her heart would ease. At the least she wouldn't have time to dwell on herself, she thought as he wheeled the ATV under the lodge's *porte cochere*.

With the sun at their backs, the pale pink marble columns turned a warm apricot. An attendant rushed to help her off the ATV, but Luciano was quicker, swinging off and offering his hand to her. She stared at the strong hand that had touched her in places no other man had with warmth and passion, well aware that refusing it was an insult.

But her pride rode strong in her now, and she needed to strike independence, if only in a small way.

"Thanks, but I can manage," she said, and got off on the side opposite of Luciano.

His lips drew into a thin line. "Very well. I'll leave you to find your room."

He swung back onto the ATV and revved the engine, shooting off like a rocket. She hadn't intended to hurt his feelings, but judging by his actions, she had.

She stood there a long moment until she could no longer see him, then strode inside the lodge, trying not to feel sorry for her actions and failing. Spite was something she never felt, but Luciano brought emotions and feelings out in her that she'd never experienced before. This one she didn't like.

When she saw him again, she'd apologize. That was all she could do at this point.

She hurried inside, but instead of seeking her room, she walked to the therapy pod. Before she chased up the design team, she wanted to have another look at the space without Luciano. He had a way of muddling her thoughts and she needed a clear head for this. If she wanted changes made to the submitted plan, it would have to be decided today.

Without Luciano's presence, the therapy pod appeared far larger. She walked the space, envisioning how each area would look and function. One certainly worked hand in hand with the other in regard to therapy, a fact she'd leaned early in her training.

Nothing appeared off, yet she couldn't shake her sense of unease. What caused it?

She stepped around the wall into the last area, which boasted a turret-like charm to it, and smothered her surprised gasp with a hand pressed to her mouth. A man sat in a wheelchair, his back to her.

Her chest tightened. She instantly recognized the impressive width of broad shoulders and the arrogant cant of his head.

"Julian," she said softly.

He wheeled the chair around and flashed her that winning smile. "I see my brother was successful in contracting you to rehabilitate me. You've wasted your time."

So he was a hard case, just as Luciano had told her. "He hired me to establish my therapy program here," she said, hoping that would ease the former athlete's resentment. "I could use your help."

Instead of responding to that lure, Julian spun the chair around and returned his gaze to the mountains. "I suppose he chose this pod for that?"

"He did."

"Groomed pistes for the cripples," he said, his tone mocking again. "Oh, wait, you prefer the term 'alternative skier.'"

"Bitterness doesn't become you, Julian," she said.

He hung his head, a muscle twitching along his jaw. "Sorry. I've had a rough day."

As had she, tacked on to a whirlwind three days with Luciano in a mountain hideaway. But she couldn't voice that. In fact she was at a loss how to reach Julian.

"*Scusa*, Jules," came a cultured masculine voice behind her, a voice that scraped along her nerves to free a memory she'd locked away.

Her breath froze in her lungs and her skin crawled. It couldn't be!

She prayed she was hearing things as she followed Julian's gaze to the newcomer. No joke, no mistake. Less than sixteen feet from her stood the man from her nightmares. The lift of his head and narrowing of his eyes were proof that he recognized her.

Run, her instincts screamed. *Hide. Get as far from this*

animal as you can. But even if she could force her feet to move, that would give him the satisfaction of intimidating her again. Worse, it would raise questions, and she wanted her attack buried in a deep, dark pit.

She wouldn't show fear and she wouldn't cower to him, no matter how hellish it was to be in the same room with this beast. And being in the same room with this animal who had raped her was pure torture.

"Mario, you remember Caprice Tregore, Luc's assistant during the World Cup in Val d'Isère?" Julian asked, and a part of her died fearing what Mario Godolphin would say.

Her former attacker's mouth curled into a cruel smile, but his dark eyes remained narrowed. "Yes, I remember Miss Tregore. How good to see you again."

She mumbled something resembling an acknowledgement.

Bastard! Had she come to his mind as much as he'd tormented her nightmares for years? She hoped not! She hoped he couldn't remember the details that haunted her.

"Tell me, Mario. Has my brother secured your firm for the completion of the therapy pod?" Julian asked, and her blood froze at the insane thought of dealing with Mario.

"We are discussing things," he said in a noncommittal tone.

A shiver rocketed through her. There was no way she would tolerate this man designing her therapy unit. But how could she express that to Luciano without telling him the ugly truth?

"Please, think about what I asked," she said, pressing a hand to Julian's shoulder before she strode out the door, hoping her attacker wouldn't follow.

She made it halfway down the corridor before she stole a look behind her. She was alone. Mario had stayed there.

Mario. He'd altered her life completely, spurring her to leave the world she had once loved.

For days, weeks, months after her rape she'd dreaded running into him again. Her phobia was so great and her pain so crippling that she'd pulled out of competition.

And she was glad she had.

Soon after her retirement and the horrific accident that removed the Duchelini brothers from the chase for gold, Mario had stepped in to dominate the ski world. It was the logical way of things.

For years, the ski world had been abuzz over the duo Italian champions. Luciano always took first place while Mario snared the second slot.

They were a one-two punch on the slopes that nobody could best. When Luciano retired from competition, Mario had a short run of being the best.

She'd been aware of his dominance in the sport, his name batted about everywhere in Colorado, unknowingly tossing coals on the pain that burned in her.

Then, within four years, he'd faded from the news, which was a relief to her. In fact, she'd never once considered that she would ever cross paths with Mario. She'd certainly never entertained the idea of working with him, even remotely.

It just wasn't possible. The idea of forcing her to do so turned her stomach.

But whether that happened or not, she would return home as soon as possible. There was no way she could stay and finish what she'd barely started, even though abandoning her job would kill all plans for her lodge.

She had to retreat to her safe zone. And abandon her dream?

No! Running away would convince Mario he'd bested

her again. But how could she stay here, knowing he could come upon her any second?

Her mind whirled with a solution as she waited for the elevator door to open, but nothing was coming to mind. Nothing except the urge to find Luciano and throw herself into his arms. Strong fingers wrapped around her arm and held tight and her heart nearly stopped.

Had Mario found her? Was she in his grip again?

She tried to twist free, panic bubbling up her throat when she couldn't break his hold. "I'll scream if you don't let go of me."

"Bella," Luciano said, enfolding her trembling body against his, pulling her into his arms. "What has terrified you so?"

How was she supposed to answer that? Certainly not with the truth, not when her attacker was in the lodge, clearly a friend of Julian's and of Luciano's as well. Dear God, what a monumental mistake she'd made aligning herself with an Italian, even if he was a man she'd started to trust again.

She wanted to be strong and push him away, presenting a brave face. Wanted so desperately to shun his comfort. But held close against his muscled chest, where she heard the steady drum of his heart, she was lost, burrowing against him like a child in a storm, tears smarting her eyes.

If only the past hadn't happened. If only...

"Come." He escorted her down the hall to his private elevator and pressed his thumb on the security pad.

"I'm okay," she said as the door swished open seconds later.

"No, you are not." He ushered her inside and punched the up button, all the while keeping her caged in his embrace.

"Really, I'm fine. Maybe I'm still jumpy over the avalanche," she said, and yet she was reluctant to let go of him.

His sigh rumbled through her. "That was a horrific experience."

She loosed a nervous laugh. "One I never wish to repeat."

He clasped her shoulders and levered her from him, his shrewd gaze scrutinizing her. "I should have refused to take you up there."

"It happened, like most accidents do. It's over. If I have flashbacks they are mine to deal with."

"As well I know," he said bitterly, looking away.

She cupped his jaw and forced his gaze back to her. It was far easier to be the inquisitor than the one questioned. "You revisit the accident again and again?"

"Playing shrink again?" he asked.

"Being a friend. I care about you," she said and thought, *far too much at times*. "I know how the bad memories can haunt you."

One dark eyebrow lifted over a discerning blue eye. "Do you?"

His doubt was understandable. And really, why had she even brought her own problems into this mix?

"I don't know what it's like to experience what you and your brother did, but my life hasn't been devoid of heartache."

He clasped her hand and pulled her close, his other hand lifting to cup the back of her head, his long fingers gently massaging at the tension that gripped. "We have both had our trials and tribulations since birth. Wealth or lack of it made no difference. Agree?"

She filled her lungs and heaved out a breath, nodding. "Agree."

"Would you like a drink? Wine? Scotch?"

Liquor was the last thing she needed, as she wanted her wits sharp as tacks, yet as wound up as she was she doubted she would find any peace this night. "Scotch but light," she said at last.

He obliged with a nod, pressing a thick glass into her hand, before raising his own. "To the launch of your therapy program worldwide."

"To your astute help achieving it," she said and clinked her glass with his.

It should be just this simple, thanks to his financial assistance on the project she'd poured long hours into. But Mario's presence changed everything. It sullied her dream and left her too skittish to concentrate.

She simply couldn't get around it. That left her one choice. Get rid of the problem or bail, and she sure didn't want to run away again.

"I spoke briefly with Julian today," she said. "He mentioned you might have hired an architect to work at the lodge."

He frowned, staring into his half empty glass. "As of this point, I haven't decided whether I should go with Godolphin's firm."

She bit her lower lip, biting back what she wanted to say. This was her problem. Not his. And yet to think that Mario Godolphin would have his name tied to any part of her program made her sick.

"I thought he was a close friend of yours," she said, as if that was reason enough to hire him for the job.

"I've known him all my life, but he is a closer friend to Julian than to me." His frown deepened. "Mario was a rival on the slopes and has proven to be a challenging businessman, branching out from his initial architectural firm."

So there was a chance to oust him. "Are there other companies you're considering?"

"Several, including the firm that built the lodge."

"Not that you asked, but I'd suggest you stick with the same firm so the design is exact instead of similar," she said, then dropped the subject before she said too much. "Have you any idea when the rest of the equipment will arrive? It's imperative we get this done as quickly and efficiently as possible."

"You're that anxious to get away from me?"

"No, I..." She just wanted to put distance between herself and her attacker. Wanted desperately to slam the door on that dark moment in her past forever. "It's complicated."

He smiled and ran a hand up her arm, creating friction that hummed in her. "Want to talk about it?"

Her words thrown back at her. She shook her head, fighting tears of frustration. Revealing her past would solve nothing.

"There's nothing to talk about," she said. "I just want to get this job over and done with and go home."

He crossed both arms over his chest and stared at her, the silence crackling between them for a long, uncomfortable moment. She looked away with a shiver, afraid he could read too much into her mind. That he could uncover her deepest secret.

"Is it me you're bent on running away from?" he asked at last.

"No." She knew as soon as his blue eyes narrowed that her quick reply had revealed too much.

"Then why? Tell me why you are so desperate to leave here."

She pressed her fingers to her forehead, feeling the first tinge of a killing headache. Wasn't her heart hurting too much for her body to tolerate more?

"Drop it, Luciano."

"No. You're not leaving this room until you tell me what has upset you."

She peered at his resolute features and thought marble statues didn't look as hard or inflexible. "You can't lock me up."

"Want to bet?"

Not on her life. "You're being totally unreasonable."

One dark eyebrow arched. "You have that desperate look of a woman ready to hide from the world."

"I do not."

"I'm not blind," he said. "What are you trying to hide from?"

Tears threatened again, but she managed to hold them back. She wouldn't cry. Wouldn't give Godolphin the satisfaction of terrorizing her waking moments as well.

"Bella," Luciano murmured as he gathered her into his embrace, her weary resistance failing to deter him. "You can tell me anything. You know this."

"Not this time. Please."

The man who'd destroyed her innocence was his friend and business associate. He was here at la Duchi Royal, waiting to hear if he'd been chosen for the job. She couldn't involve Luciano in the mess that was her personal life.

And just admitting that loosed her tears. They came hot and miserably fast, burning trails of makeup down her cheeks that his tailored shirt soaked up.

"What happened? You must tell me that much," he insisted, keeping her encased within his arms, clearly not about to give up.

What was the use in holding her silence? He was right. She could tell him that much.

She sucked in a shaky breath and held it, willing the chills to stop yet knowing nothing would ever truly purge her of the hell she'd endured.

There was only one way to get through this. Tell the truth.

One more shaky inhalation and she blurted out, "I was raped."

CHAPTER SEVEN

LUC GRABBED HER forearms and held her in front of him, stunned—no, furious this horrible thing had happened to her. Rape. It was an ugly word depicting an abhorrent act. "When?"

"Years ago," she said.

"How many years?" he persisted.

She pinched her eyes shut and held her breath for several counts he was sure. "Seven."

"Seven?" The same year…as the last World Cup. Around the same time as his and Julian's accident. "Where did this happen, Caprice? How?"

"What difference does it make?"

"Tell me," he demanded.

Tears stung her eyes and she tried to wrench free, but he wasn't deterred, holding her close. "If you must know, it was a date gone horribly wrong at the World Cup. He was convinced I'd agreed to go out with him for sex, and turned deaf ears when I told him no. The next thing I knew he dragged me into an equipment storeroom and took what he wanted."

"You should have told me."

A reddish stain streaked up her neck and dotted her cheeks. "I couldn't come to you. You'd rejected me earlier that night."

He banged a fist on the door, furious he'd played a part in her turning to another and bitten with guilt that she'd thought her only recourse to take was to run away. "Did you at least summon the authorities?"

"And tell them what? Do you think they would believe me or assume I'd simply drank too much and changed my mind about having a quickie because I assure you that is exactly what *he* would have claimed," she said, her body trembling and her teary eyes stark with fear.

"So you just gave up?" he asked, ravenous for revenge and sickening fury eating at his insides.

"I was shamed beyond belief. And so terrified he'd come back and do it again," she said, tears streaming down her face, shoulders slumping. "That's why I left that night without saying a word to anyone."

"Mio Dio!" He stalked the perimeter of his office, furious this happened to her, disgusted that her attacker had never been brought to justice. That was something he intended to change. "Who the hell is he?"

"Why do you care? You dismissed me that night, wanting nothing more to do with me," she snapped back.

He slashed a hand through the air and swore again. "I turned you away because of that kiss. You touched something in me that I refused to explore further. My life was in such a turmoil then."

She blinked, eyes bright with moisture that he wanted to wipe away. Wipe away all her hurts, but he couldn't. "I wish I would have known that then. Wish I wouldn't have attempted to prove I was desirable to a man."

"As do I." He drove his fingers through his hair and swore, feeling the weight of guilt bear down on him again. "We can't change the past, but we can learn from it."

"A saying my father repeated often," she said, shaking her head, wide gaze lifting to his again. "I certainly learned the hard way about blindly trusting a man."

He took her cold hands in his, hating the shiver that coursed through her, hating her attacker more with each breath. "Bella, tell me his name. Let me settle this for you."

She shook her head violently. "It doesn't matter."

He gave her one terse shake. "It matters to me. Is there a connection between your attack and your aversion to remaining here?"

Her gaze lowered, her skin paling. "There isn't one."

He swore roundly again. "I don't believe you. You have seen him here, perhaps have spoken with him. Is he a guest? Employee? Someone who lives in the village? Tell me."

"Stop it, Luciano. What happened was in the past. Let it go."

His palms cupped her face, holding her still, as he kissed the tears from her cheeks. "I will not give up until you tell me his name."

Her shoulders slumped and her head bowed. "It was Mario."

"Mario Godolphin?" he asked, and at her nod, he dropped his hold on her, fingers bunched into fists, his rage towering higher than the mountains. "I'll kill him."

"No!" She gripped his wrists, complexion growing deathly pale. "Please, Luciano, I want that entire ugly night to remain forgotten."

"Why? You've never forgotten it," he said. "Even if you had, Mario laid his filthy hands on you. He hurt you. Now he must pay for those actions."

She tipped her head back and growled low in her throat. "It is his word against mine and I refuse to go into battle with a man who will deliberately make me look like I pursued him," she said, hysteria rising in her voice. "That publicity is too humiliating to face, let alone endure."

He combed his fingers though his hair and swore, sickened that he'd failed another person he cared about. If there was a chance he could make this right for her... If he could undo a wrong and bring someone to justice, he damned well would.

"You can't let him get away with this violation," he said.

"It is my choice to make," she said, voice cracking.

Had she ever felt this raw and exposed and rigorously furious? No, not even after the rape, after she'd fled home to Colorado, after she'd gone through weeks of worry until she was certain she wasn't pregnant.

This time she wasn't just fighting for her sanity and career. She was fighting for her independence, even though that hard-won gem might sever her from Luciano forever. But the business deal she struck with him and their affair would end soon anyway. She had to take this stand.

"Don't you see that if I *deny* anything happened between us, it diminishes Mario's hold over me?" she asked, desperate for him to understand her fears and phobias. "It gives me the power to choose."

He stared at her a long hard moment before he stalked to the window and stood with his broad back to her, which for all the world seemed an impenetrable wall. She resisted the impulse to cross to him and wrap her arms around his waist.

"What can I do to make this right for you?" he asked.

If only he could... "I need to know if Mario's firm is vital to la Duchi Royal."

He pulled a dark face. "It is true he's been the exclusive architect on all my projects."

She pressed a hand to her queasy stomach, her blood chilling. "He'll continue working with you then, right here."

"No. I am done with him."

Bubbles of panic popped inside her. "But if you sever ties with Mario now, he'll know I told you what happened."

"Who cares what he thinks?" he asked.

"I do and so should you. Think what he will do if you break your contract with him," she said. "There are legalities to face, and what about the ensuing publicity?"

"Mario won't be so foolish as to engage in a legal battle with me," he said.

She hugged herself but still couldn't stop her trembling. "What if you're wrong? What if he retaliates and spreads vicious lies about me? I can't have that black mark attached to my name or my program."

"I respect your decision to keep silent about this, but your way of dealing with it is to live in denial—and whilst that is your choice, I intend to take the direct and final approach." He snagged the phone off his desk. "Get legal on the phone now."

Panic clawed at her throat. "If you go through with this now, I'll be the one who'll end up with the tainted reputation."

"I won't allow that to happen." He slashed the air with his hand, features hard and cold. He spoke into the receiver. "Begin proceedings today to cancel all contracts with Mario Godolphin in all industries and business." He paused, listening for a response. "Yes, every single one of them, and see that he's barred from setting foot at this lodge."

He soundlessly laid the receiver in the cradle, but a black silence roared in the room.

She pressed her palms to her temples, chest heaving, her control close to snapping like a mighty pine under the force of an avalanche. "I've worked hard all of my life to ensure I had a clean name. Divulging the past now will ruin that. They'll believe every lie he tells."

He chewed out a curse, muscle thrumming madly in his lean cheek, eyes narrowed to angry slits. "And what if letting him get away with this leads him to force himself on another woman?"

She covered her face with her palms, feeling sick inside. Trapped. "I would never want this to happen to any woman."

"Neither do I," he said. "Severing all ties with Godolphin is the right thing for me to do. You must choose what you feel is the right thing to do for yourself. But, *bella,* Mario is the guilty party in this. He should be held accountable for harming you."

She sighed, so very tired of running, hiding, of closeting her emotions so they wouldn't leave her vulnerable to making the same mistake again. "Okay," she said at last. "I'll consider it, after my contract is completed."

"Good."

He crossed to an elaborate liquor cabinet, but instead of fixing a drink, he stood there like a statue. She wondered what to do. If there was anything she could or should do.

Hesitantly, she crossed to him and wrapped her arms around his stiff frame, desperate to feel his strength. To hide from reality if just a little while longer.

He remained cold and hard as steel for less than a heartbeat in her embrace. Then he heaved a sigh, grasped her wrists to stay her and turned to embrace her so tightly she feared she might break. She grabbed a breath, then another and held it tightly as his arms enveloped her, holding her close, his head finding a place on her shoulder to rest, his face millimeters from her neck with his breath so intensely hot that her chills finally, *finally* eased.

"I'm sorry," she whispered at last.

"Why? You've done nothing wrong," he said. "You're the one wronged by me and an old friend, damn his soul."

"It was partly my fault. I knew better, but I did it anyway," she said. "Let it go, Luciano. Retaliation isn't the answer."

"This is not your decision to make."

Panic stabbed through her like fallen icicles piercing the snow. "Isn't it? Your name is golden. It can withstand bad press. Mine can't, not when I'm so close to launching my program worldwide."

He fisted his hands at his sides, jaw rigid. "I can't let this go. He's hurt you because I failed you. A revelation of this scope could protect innocents, or at the very least shine light on his crime. And you are tied to me through our mutual contract. If he besmears our names, my attorneys will have him tied up in legalities in an hour or less."

She grabbed a breath, frustration pinching her soul, wanting this lifted from her conscience. He was right and she hated him for it. She wasn't selfish. The truth could protect women from Mario, but the consequences of having everyone know her own personal nightmare scared her to death.

"I don't know if I'm strong enough to face this," she said honestly.

"You aren't," he said, stepping closer, his strong arms coming around her. "Not alone. I'll be with you. Yes, there will be gossip tossed about, but I promise it will not have any ill effect on your lodge."

She rested her forehead on his chest, but his heat couldn't thaw the deep chill invading her soul. "How can you possibly promise that?" she asked, her deep fears sleeping just under the surface.

He pressed his lips to her forehead, her eyes, and nuzzled her head up to brush his lips over hers once, twice. "We will marry. He wouldn't dare sully your name then."

"What?" she squeaked, too stunned to make sense of his out-of-the-blue proposal. "You don't love me."

"Love," he muttered, shaking his head. "Our marriage would be a contract. You'd be under my protection with full access to a battery of la Duchi attorneys."

He was offering another business arrangement, only this one with sex. It certainly wasn't a marriage and wasn't for her, simply because love wasn't involved and never would be, at least not mutually. His heart would never be hers because he'd given it to his wife long ago, and she had taken it with her to her grave.

"Why are you doing this?" she asked.

"I failed to protect you the first time."

"I wasn't yours to protect," she said.

Not that his reasons or rationale mattered. There wouldn't be a sham marriage for her. She would have to be crazy or desperate or both to put herself through an emotional hell that would take her years to recover from. *If* she ever recovered.

"*Bella*, be reasonable."

"No! I refuse to marry under those circumstances," she said and headed for the door and fresh air. Freedom.

She would rather be alone and in control of her life than enter into a marriage of convenience.

"Don't reject this out of hand," he said.

"If you'll excuse me, I've got work to do," she said, and walked from his office with her head high and her heart heavy.

She'd rejected him. Rejected him.

For days the thought had haunted him. He was, in a sense, off the hook. Relief should wash over him instead of these needles of anxiety. He should brush it off instead of dwelling on her refusal. But he couldn't.

Annoyance pinged his taut nerves as he crossed to the window and stared out at the hard, unyielding mass of mountains, feeling cold and remote inside. This sense of aloofness closing around him wasn't new. He'd gladly embraced it after his divorce. He'd worn it like a shield, never wishing to cast it off.

He liked his life the way it was, without commitment, without a woman complicating his life. He'd proposed to Caprice to protect her. That's all.

Yet she'd refused him. And his protection.

He blew out a long sigh and hung his head, determined to get back on track. For weeks he'd tried to put Caprice in the same class as Isabella, out to get his money and entrée his name would lend. But she was nothing like his ex-wife.

Caprice had abided by the letter of their contract.

He would not complain about that.

She wanted a premier facility in Colorado and he would see that she got it. He could see now that she wanted to enjoy sex with him.

It had been good. Amazing for him. But was she able to say the same?

His intercom beeped. "Sorry to bother you, Luc, but you wanted to know when the therapy equipment had been set up."

"Thank you, Eva."

In a matter of minutes, he arrived at the therapy pod for a quick inspection, frowning as resonant clicks and whirs echoed from deep in the unit. Was someone using the equipment unsupervised?

He crossed to the sounds coming from the far room, only to pull back around the privacy wall. Julian was strapped into a harness that allowed him to stand on a massive machine while Caprice supervised.

"That's it," she said. "Stretch slow and steady again, holding when you reach the point of peak endurance."

A masculine grunt, then a loud clank. "I can't do this."

Luc peered around the corner, careful to remain hidden. The defeat on his brother's face stabbed at his heart. And then he looked at Caprice and saw the compassion glittering in her eyes as she patiently readjusted the straps on the pulleys and handed the ends to Julian.

"'Can't' isn't a word we use here," she said softly, pressing a palm to Julian's muscled bicep, as if encouraging him to try again. "It's going to pull, hurt and resist. You have to work at this. You have to want it."

Julian gave a short nod and began using the equipment again, face contorting as he exerted upper body strength. Slowly, minutely, his legs began moving back and forth, mimicking the motion of cross-country skiing.

Julian barked a laugh and Luc smiled. "I can't believe it. As my legs are worked, the tension in my shoulders eases."

"That's because your entire body is moving as it should in motion," she said. "You're doing great. But another minute then you stop for today, okay?"

"No problem. We'll do this again tomorrow, right?"

"Right," she said.

Luc stood there a moment longer, watched the satisfaction on Caprice's face reflected from the serious intent of Julian's. She wasn't all talk and no action. She was the perfect package, doing just as she said she would for his brother by implementing her unique program with specialized equipment.

Absently he rubbed the weak area of his leg. Was there a chance she could help him as well? Probably so, but he wasn't going to think of himself or of his brother.

Right now was about Caprice. He wanted to return the favor, do something special just for her.

A moment later he knew just what that would be. He would give her a night to remember. The perfect night she'd been denied.

Toward dusk, Luc strode down the executive hallway, a box of Noka chocolates and a bottle of Dom Perignon vintage brut champagne in one hand and a bloodred rose in the other. If it looked like an apology, so be it.

He hadn't been able to think of anything else, other than a diamond ring and undying professions of love, that would embody *amore* better than what he'd chosen. Besides, after his divorce, he'd vowed he would never risk his heart on a woman again.

So he decided to shower Caprice with romance. Indulge her passions. Prove to her she was a very desirable woman whom he respected and wanted.

He didn't count the sultry nights spent in each other's arms, indulging in sex. He certainly didn't want to revisit that first time, which had been a rushed, frenzied affair.

Every sexual encounter they'd shared had come before he'd known about her attack.

It became clear to him then that she deserved to be pampered and indulged. Made love to deeply and passionately, focusing on her wants and needs and desires instead of his own.

Which is what had brought him here bearing romantic gifts.

He rapped on her door, gripped with an odd nervousness he hadn't felt in years. Perhaps because doing this for her meant so much to him.

This was to be her night of decadent indulgence. This was to be the one she would remember instead of the painful one, and the harried times they'd made love. This would be the time that she was given all and expected to do nothing but savor each moment.

She swung the door open, her smile a bit uncertain. "You're right on time."

"And you are lovely," he said, visually caressing the blue dress that draped her full bosom before nipping in at her waist to hug her from hips to hem.

"Thanks. You look amazingly handsome as always," she said.

"For you." He handed her the rose and chocolates before lifting the bottle. "I thought this would be an excellent time to have a pre-celebration drink to toast the near completion of our therapy pod."

"Good idea. The work has been intense the past week but well worth the effort," she said, taking a leisurely inhalation of the rose and smiling. "Wow! I never expected this. Thank you, Luciano."

"My pleasure." He motioned her to precede him into the sitting room and waited until she'd chosen a seat, hiding his surprise and relief when she eased onto the sofa.

He uncorked the champagne, splashed some in two crystal flutes and joined her. "I've taken the liberty of reserving a table for us in the village."

She took the glass, her smile fading. "I'm not sure I'm up for going out tonight."

He moved closer and slipped an arm around her shoulders. "Are you worried you will run into Mario?"

She shrugged, staring at her lap, reverting to the restrained woman he preferred not to see tonight. "A bit."

"You won't find him here or in the village," he said, drawing her close and dropping a kiss on her forehead. "But if you really don't wish to go out, we can dine in. Your choice, *bella*."

Her brow puckered and she fidgeted with her fingers, her body far too tense to find pleasure in anything right now. "I won't let that man keep me a prisoner here or anywhere else. You've made the reservation so let's go."

He lifted his glass to hers, marveling again at this woman he'd underestimated. "Well said, *bella*. You are strong. Smart. Beautiful. To you and all you wish for."

"And you as well," she replied, clinking her glass to his, her smile quivering the slightest bit, as if she were fighting tears.

But she wouldn't cry. He knew that much about her. This moment didn't warrant tears. Within fifteen minutes they arrived at the *ristorante* in his limo and were promptly escorted to a private nook. The space was small and the lighting subdued. *Perfecto!*

Luc assisted her to her chair and took his own, still struggling with that odd sense of imbalance. "I've ordered a pinot grigio, but if you prefer something else…"

"That would be heavenly," she said, looking relaxed.

He tasted the wine and accepted it, then asked for a selection of appetizers, gaining Caprice's okay, which again came readily. And wasn't that exactly one of the things he liked most about her? They were in sync on preferred designs, adventurous palettes and the hunger of carnal pleasures, the latter being what he wished to explore leisurely with her tonight.

His wish was for her to walk away from him and Italy feeling very much in control of her mind and fully attuned to the needs and provocative charms of her body. Together they were a powerful aphrodisiac possessing the power to bring him down to his knees.

He jerked when her hand pressed over his. "Is everything okay?"

"Yes, fine," he said, closing the door on emotions stirring to escape.

His feelings had no place here. This was her night. The one she'd deserved from him seven years ago.

"I want this to be a good night you will recall with pleasure," he said. "Would you prefer a menu?"

She leaned back in her chair, her glass cradled in her hands, her gaze drinking him as if she were parched. "It seems you've designed this night for me. You decide, Luciano."

"To your pleasure," he said, just barely tipping his glass to her and liking this surety and boldness about her.

My God, he admired her strength. Whatever it took he would make this night very special for her.

They dined on a medley of vegetables, cheese and crusty breads reminiscent of Austria, and he placed their entrées along with another bottle of wine.

"This is fabulous," she said, scooping a generous portion of *parmesano polenta* dressed with wild mushrooms, sausage and tomatoes onto crusty bread.

She held it out, tempting him to lean close, to take it from her fingers.

And he did. Slowly. Ending with a swish of his tongue over pale skin that tasted sweet. "Delicious," he said.

Her tongue flicked over her lush lips; then she leaned forward, her grin challenging, her eyes sparkling with devilment. "My turn."

That remark crumbled any remaining awkwardness lingering between them. They ate. They drank. They flirted outrageously.

When the generous plate of carpaccio of beef and greens arrived, they laughed and ate and drank and let go, enjoying the moment. Laughter grew softer as did the few words spoken. And through it all the wine flowed.

"What is your dream?" he asked her when the plates were cleared and the dessert they would barely touch had been ordered.

She smiled and laughed, but the exuberance was gone. "Part of me will always long for a home and family. Normalcy. But with my career—" She shook her head, her laugh far too brief. "You were my dream, Luciano. Nothing will ever compare so I will never try. But would I anyway? You've made sure my career is set. I can't complain. Ever."

But did she want to? "You humble me when I don't deserve it."

"But you do." She looked away, pensive. "We come from different lives. Different wants and dreams. We end when the job ends because we must."

"Yes," he said, nodding yet unsettled she'd grasped what was obvious so easily. "You're right. It is the only way. So let's make the most of this night."

"I couldn't agree more."

The decadent dessert was left, as was an uncorked and untried bottle of wine. Luciano clasped her to his side and ushered her to the limo, pulling her into his arms.

"That was so good, so good," she said, lifting her face to his, her fingers tracing long, lazy figure eights on his back.

In what seemed a blip in time, they reached his lodge. "We'll take the back elevator up to my suite," he said, guiding her into the lift.

"You're just full of surprises," she said, pulling away from him and stepping back from the glass enclosure that offered a bird's-eye view of the lodge and the Alps.

He laughed. "It is one-way glass, *bella*. Come," he said when the doors whispered open.

In a moment, they were secluded in his suite. He pulled her into his arms, backing her into his bedroom, ravenous to taste her, to get drunk from her kisses.

His lips found hers in a melding of lips and tongues that was pure carnal abandonment. Hands joined in, lifting her onto his massive bed and following her down, fingers sneaking beneath the constraints of clothes, finding flesh that was hot and wet and wanting.

"Yes," she breathed when his forefinger skimmed the heat of her core while his thumb found pleasure point.

"Oh, God," she moaned, arching her back, shivering with desire.

He peeled her thong away and pushed her skirt up, wanting only to pleasure her. Taste her. With seductive precision, he opened her to him with his tongue and finger before he thrust inside her, playing a game with her libido and his own, gambling which one of them could hold out. God, he could draw this moment out. Embed memories of a night that would never be triumphed.

She would remember her first lover, the first encounter with sex not counting because it had been taken. This was given to her.

He clasped her buttocks as she arched her back, surrendering the passion locked in her. So sweet. So tight. His gift.

What they shared was a moment she would bank away for the future if loneliness overcame her. He hoped she would remember the very good and not the bad, that those images of a beast abusing her would vanish. God knew he would banish them for good if he could.

Caprice was just rousing from her climax, supine and drowsy in his arms.

"That was beyond wonderful," she said. "Now I believe it is your turn."

He caught her before she could move, drinking from her lips until he was drunk on passion, until his own plans of setting her away from him seemed flawed.

"You make leaving difficult," she said.

"I could say the same."

Their mouths met and melded again in a moan, lips dueling an erotic melody while their hips swayed to the same wanton rhythm. Whatever time they had together, he would give her his all. He wouldn't regret this decision.

She deserved this from him and so much more.

And yet was this lovemaking that much different?

Yes, because his attitude was different. He'd given without expecting compensation.

Her head lulled back, a sigh whispering from her. "I feel boneless," she said, clearly basking in the sensations rocking through her while he did the same just knowing he'd given her this release.

He pulled her flush against him, the hard length of his erection pressed to her belly as he kissed her neck before his lips found her ear and his tongue traced the contours, pleasuring her until she cried his name. Only then did he look up into her face and catch her wide smile of pleasure.

And he smiled, knowing he'd succeeded, that she had indulged in passion. *Remember me*, he thought before he tucked her close and sought the same sleep she was quickly falling into.

CHAPTER EIGHT

CAPRICE STRETCHED IN the massive bed, silk sheet under her bosom, her mind clearing from the sensual haze she'd reveled in last night. Talk had been minimal after that last amazing joining of bodies and souls, or at least it had felt that strong and good for her.

Now her affair was closing. Luciano had said so in so many words. But she didn't balk. She had to get away from here and return home so she was grounded. Had to get away to where the likelihood of running into Mario was incredibly small.

She could manage. She had in the past seven years.

The bathroom door opened and he stalked inside, looking painfully contemplative. "What's wrong?"

"I need to return to Colorado," she said.

He swore and stormed toward her, towel cinched over his lean hips. "Why?" he said with a dismissive wave of his hand. "It would be safer if you stayed here awhile longer."

"Where I could run into Mario at any time?"

"I've barred him from coming to the lodge."

"But you can't keep him out of the village." She stared at the intricate swirls of blue and red that outlined the exquisite black geometric designs in the Turkish carpet, waiting for him to deny it. But he couldn't because it was true. "I can't stay here."

"Can't or won't?"

She signed, not wishing to delve into this discussion on the tail end of a marvelous night of celebration. "Won't. This isn't just about Mario. If I'm to make a success of my business, I need to complete my work here and return to Colorado."

He cupped her chin and forced her to look at him. Had blue eyes ever seemed so intense? This assertive? "The lodge isn't finished yet. Where will you go?"

She pulled back from the touch that felt too comforting and the eyes that probed far too deeply. "I have friends in Colorado that I can stay with until the lodge renovations are completed."

"You're certain?" Luciano asked, jaw set tight.

"Yes. As soon as my work here is done, I'll go home."

The following week Caprice saw little of Luciano. It was unbelievable how the time had zipped past in a flurry of last-minute details she had to attend to on the therapy pod. The grand opening was a week away. The first therapy guests would arrive in a few days.

She would return home to stay with friends. Yes, staying here in Italy would be easier, but wasn't that the problem? Everything she experienced here with Luciano wasn't real.

It wasn't love.

It wasn't commitment.

What they had together here was amazing sex. Nothing more.

That wasn't enough to keep her here. In fact it was the very reason she should go. Leaving here would break this addiction she had for Luciano and force her to take back control of her life and business.

She slid from the bed and slipped into a lovely satin robe

that had appeared the day she'd arrived. More clothes had been delivered since then. All were his choice. All were far too elegant for her to wear when she returned to Colorado and the real world. But for now they suited the role she was playing.

She walked barefoot into the adjacent salon where the *colazione* had been deposited on the sideboard. After pouring a cup of *caffè e latte* and selecting a *brioche,* she curled up on the divan just as the bedroom door opened and Luciano strode into the room, his lean muscled body bare except for a thick, knotted towel that rode low on his lean hips.

A different hunger stirred inside her until her gaze lifted to his remote features. "Is something wrong?"

"We need to talk," he said, pouring a rich coffee for himself before joining her on the divan with masculine grace.

"Sounds serious. Please tell me this has nothing to do with my lodge," she said, hoping she hadn't suffered any setbacks there.

He gave one abrupt shake of his head and stared at her with eyes that burned with fury. "My PA rang me yesterday. Mario scheduled a press conference in Milan tomorrow. According to sources he wants to set the record straight on why la Duchi has halted his company from further work at the lodge."

The bite of sweet brioche she'd just eaten soured in her stomach. "I was afraid he would defy any threat."

"He is an arrogant fool," he said. "I will not allow him to spew lies."

"There must be some other way to silence Mario. A payoff, maybe?" she asked, desperate to avoid scandal.

"He has money to burn. But he does rely heavily on the endorsement he's always gotten from being the architect of my projects, several that were still in the planning stage," he said, challenge darkening his eyes to a stormy blue. "Once legal measures are finalized and his current contracts with la Duchi are nullified, many businessmen will notice and follow suit, not wishing to do business with his sort."

"Do you really think you can ruin him?" she asked, not entirely convinced he wielded that much power.

He pulled her close and kissed her hard, possessively. "Yes. Trust me, *bella*."

"I do." At least she was trying to put all her faith in him.

"Continue with the plans here. I'll return before the opening. Promise," he said, and when she nodded he released her and found his clothes.

She allowed herself the pleasure of watching him thrust long legs into snug black jeans, the denim hugging his firm thighs and riding low on his lean hips. He pulled on a gray jersey and tugged it over the muscled slabs of his chest, tucking it in with an economy of movement.

Her heart swelled, even though sadness lurked in the back of her mind. He was hers to physically love for a week more at most. For the umpteenth time she asked herself if this heaven she reveled in now was worth the hell she'd sink into when they separated.

The answer was obvious. She was a career girl. She was determined to be independent of a man.

She could survive alone. But did she really want to?

No. But her relationship with Luciano was drawing to an end. The most she could hope for was a few more nights with him as his lover. Having her own business and being self-sufficient was what she had dreamed of for years. So why did she entertain doubts about every facet of her life?

"Are you all right?" he asked, startling her.

"I'm anxious about the grand opening for the therapy unit at your lodge."

"It will be fine. Perfect," he said. "You will be as well."

"I hope you're right."

She crossed to him with a smile and wrapped her arms around his neck, tilting her face to his, for the first time offering herself to him for whatever he wished to do. His sudden stiffening froze her to the spot.

"What's wrong?" she asked.

"My thoughts are on dealing with Mario," he said, grasping her wrists and gently setting her aside. "We'll talk at length when I return."

He strode out the door without a goodbye or kiss, his curt rejection cutting like a knife, bringing back unpleasant memories of how he'd been too involved in competition to have much courtesy for anything or anyone, especially her. How easily he'd dismissed her back then.

But then she'd been nothing but the volunteer helper. The starry-eyed young woman who'd had a too-big crush for the champion.

And now? She shook her head, admitting she hadn't escaped that yet. Sure she was his business associate as well as his convenient lover. But once the contract was finished, all of that would end.

It was what she wanted. What she'd demanded from the start. So she shouldn't feel melancholy now.

Luciano was never going to change, so it was useless to continue trying.

For the first time in weeks, she knew exactly what she had to do. After the grand opening at his lodge, she would return to Colorado and begin the lengthy process of putting him from her mind.

Hours later, Luc landed his private Eurocopter atop his towering glass and steel office building in Milano. He still got a special thrill seeing the helo's reflection on the structure's sides. This was his baby. The pinnacle of taking a million-dollar business that had gone stale and expanding it into a multibillion-dollar corporation.

He'd done it in less than a decade, which was much more than Mario could boast.

Mario. The detectives he'd hired confirmed his old friend had stayed in Milano, living and working out of his office. The fact he'd gotten away with rape still filled him with rage. But it wasn't his place to bring that revelation to the public.

Only one person could do that. Caprice. So far she wasn't inclined to do so.

He pounded across the helipad to the rooftop door, recalling the last time he'd rushed here on business was the morning after his ex-wife's fatal accident. The tabloids had been filled with truths and half-truths and lies.

Guilt had nipped at him for ending their marriage so swiftly. For giving her no chance to explain or apologize.

But that guilt wasn't near as biting as what he felt for the sweet young attendant he'd hired at the World Cup in Val d'Isère. Caprice had done everything he'd asked and anticipated his needs to the heartbeat. And she'd fallen into puppy love with him—a dog of a man.

Instead of putting her down gently, he'd dismissed her in the same manner he would fire a lazy employee. All because her kiss had stirred feelings in him that he'd only felt for his wife. The tender emotions that were a prequel to love.

That realization had scared the hell out of him. He'd vowed never to love again. Never to give his heart to another. He could not risk being around her.

So he'd left her vulnerable. And his friend Mario—*his damned friend, of all people!*—had taken advantage of her.

Luc remembered his treks down to the caretaker's house

to tempt Mario away from his chores. They'd been closer than brothers for years.

Before Luc had begun training vigorously for Alpine, he'd convinced his father to pay for Mario's way. They'd been an unbeatable duo on the slopes, and pursued by countless women across the globe.

But that had changed as well after the accident. Mario had remained in his life as a friend, and if not for Caprice's tearful confession, he never would have known the depths Mario was capable of sinking to.

Luc drove his fingers through his hair and swore. He would not repeat past mistakes and cause Caprice more grief. The fact he'd done so years ago made it even more difficult for him to face himself in the mirror. And to think he'd thought his father was a careless bastard!

The American saying "the apple doesn't fall far from the tree" certainly was true in Luc's case. He wasn't worthy of tying himself to a good woman. He'd already screwed up badly two times. He wouldn't do so a third time.

Caprice had done everything they'd agreed to. She'd established her premier program at his lodge, and she'd thankfully incited his brother's interest in life again.

The renovation he'd begun at her lodge in Colorado paled in comparison. She deserved much more.

He would see she received a hefty settlement so she would never want for money. So she could move forward with her life without financial worry. So he couldn't hurt her more. Then he would never trouble her again.

His driver was waiting below and made a quick twenty-minute drive to Mario's firm across the city. With instructions to his driver to wait, Luc exited his luxury Mercedes and marched into the Godolphin building Mario had designed and built from the ground up.

The express elevator sped him to the thirty-fifth floor

and a modicum of steps took him to Mario's outer office. "Signor Duchelini!" Mario's PA said, shooting to her feet. "Is Mario expecting you?"

"No," he said, storming past her. "It is a surprise visit."

He twisted the knob and entered his old friend's lair, slamming the door in the PA's face and twisting the lock, ensuring privacy. "Cancel your press conference."

Mario lounged in his chair and laced his fingers over his flat stomach, a sly grin touching his hard mouth. "A man must defend his honor."

"Don't speak to me about honor. You have none."

Mario sat up, sobering. "So you take the word of a woman and take legal measures to nullify Godolphin contracts with all la Duchi holdings."

"She told me what happened. Why did you do it?" Luc asked, desperate to know what had corrupted Mario's mind.

Mario leaped to his feet, dark eyes slitted and sweat dotting his upper lip. "You've got this all wrong. Caprice came to me. She asked for it."

He barely restrained himself from driving his fist into his old friend's face. "Enough lies! I'll never forgive myself for tossing her out of my life, leaving her vulnerable for a shark like you. I won't make that mistake again."

Mario had the gall to laugh. "Don't play martyr or gallant over a woman you hold no affection toward."

That remark was sharper than a knife that sank deep, drawing emotional blood. "I'm not leaving myself blameless, but I was your friend. You used an innocent girl!"

"How interesting that young girl is now your mistress. I've never known you to defend one before. Hell, you wouldn't do that for your wife."

"Don't ever speak ill of either woman again," he said, jabbing a finger at the man he now considered his enemy.

"I know you raped Caprice. Why, Mario? Why did you do it?"

Mario sneered and his eyes went jet black. "You're a rich boy with a family legacy on the slopes and everything you wanted at your fingertips. Not once did you or your family hide the fact I was the charity cause you took on. The 'friend' most saw as a hanger-on. No matter how I tried, you always won the top medals, secured the richest business deals and toyed with the most beautiful women. But I finally bested you. I had your sweet little American first."

Luc lunged across the desk, grabbed him by the collar and jerked him back across the desk, holding him so close that the red streaks in Mario's eyes stood out in bold relief. "If I ever catch you on any Duchelini holding or if you dare make any of our conversation public, I will come after you with enough legal guns to destroy you."

He shoved Mario away from him and stalked out the door. A few months ago he would have sought release of his rage through drink and a willing woman. Now his only thought was returning to Caprice.

But he had urgent business to settle here with his lawyers that would take days. He had to ensure Mario would never be a threat to any woman again. He had to safeguard Caprice.

No matter what it took, he couldn't fail her a second time.

"Yes, that's it," Caprice said, more to herself than the two workers.

It had been a hectic week ensuring everything was in place and going as planned, watching her advertisements go up in the newspapers and on television. Though she'd hoped for a good turnout, she hadn't expected she would get such a crowd. But Luciano's PA informed her that the lodge was booked to capacity for the grand opening.

Now, as the finishing touches were put into place, she stood aside, fingers entwined under her chin, watching, stomach alight with butterflies. Even after the workers slipped out the pod door, she didn't move, preferring to admire the high intensity of this room used for those almost ready to hit the slopes again. From the vibrant splashes of color on the walls to the living backdrop of rugged mountains capped with snow and the challenging green runs lying in wait for that first blanket of snow beyond the bay of windows…it was spectacular.

Her eyes misted and her heart swelled as the vision she'd dreamed of for years came to life before her eyes. "It's absolutely perfect."

"So are you," Luciano said, startling her.

She whirled to face him, cursing the fact her cheeks were flaming and her hands and knees trembled with that giddy excitement that still hit her whenever he was near. "When did you get back?"

"Just now. I came straight here."

"You look exhausted," she said, afraid to ask how it went, afraid that the news wouldn't be good.

Too much had gone right lately for her to believe it would continue. Her luck had never lasted that long.

He shrugged. "It's only been a week, but I've been assured that Mario's clients are dropping at a steady rate."

"He must be frantic. Furious with you. Me."

"Tough. He deserves to wallow in his own hell."

She bit her lip, agreeing but worried just the same. "Is there a chance he still might go to the press?"

"Sure, but he's a fool if he does." He straddled a weight bench, tested the pulleys and whistled. "These are good strength trainers."

"Thanks," she said, knowing she couldn't dwell on Mario and his threats with the opening tomorrow—with the man she loved here before her. "I designed these to build upper-body strength needed for downhill and endurance."

He tested them again and nodded. "Mind if I avail myself of them?"

"Anytime," she said with a smile, stepping close enough to smooth a hand over his muscled shoulder. "It's good to see you again."

He was off the bench and gathering her close in a heartbeat, lips closing over hers for one long, lusty kiss that chased her earlier weariness away. "It is good to be back with you as well, *bella*. A man could get used to this."

So could she. The question remained, should she? "So what happened? You know I've been on needles and pins since you left."

"Mario denied any wrongdoing, but I didn't buy his lies this time," he said, sobering far too much for her liking. "I served him the papers severing all contracts with Godolphin and walked out."

Could it be that final? Was she finally free of any threat from Mario?

"It's over then? I can go on with my life?"

He nodded and ran his palms up and down her back, his touch both soothing and erotic. "Is that what you want, *bella*?"

"Of course. It's what I've worked for," she said and smiled, only to sober when he didn't return the gesture. "The preparations for the opening of your therapy unit are completed as well. In fact they delivered the sign this afternoon."

"Excellent. Have you looked at it yet?" he asked, his beetled brow hinting he'd expected her to do just that.

She shook her head. "No. I told the workers to place the sign in the hall leading to the ski exit. I didn't think it would be in the way there." And it was less tempting.

"Let's take a look then."

He took her hand and led her to the hallway and the large covered sign that would hang over the glass doors of the pod. In seconds he ripped the heavy brown paper from the sign, then stepped back.

"Do you like it?" he asked.

She stared at it, stunned, not having expected or demanded her name be tied with his lodge. But it was here, large and bold. Another tie binding them.

"Caprice Tregore's Adaptive Ski Therapy and Sports Medicine," she read, her gaze flicking back to her larger-than-life initials in a casual script above the bold print to the smaller trio at the bottom of certificates and degrees she'd earned. "I didn't expect this."

"I commissioned two. One for my lodge and the other for yours," he said. "It is crucial we keep the continuity of the brand."

"Yes, consistency of my program is crucial," she said. "But why put such emphasis on my name?"

He slipped an arm around her shoulders, his laugh echoing free and clear and so welcome to her ears. "Your name is your brand. When people see this sign, they will know that this is the quality care and commitment they need."

She considered that compliment with a frown. "Like athletes with their endorsements?"

"Far more powerful and important than that." He kissed her forehead, her eyes, her cheeks, his splayed palm firm against her back, holding her flush against him—not that she needed that urging. "Athletes' accolades are the result of skill and luck. You are a trained professional who has earned the respect of physicians, therapists and athletes. You change lives for the better."

She buried her face against his chest, reveling in his spicy scent and strength. "You make me sound far more important than I am."

"Bella," he said, nudging her chin up. "That is your charm—you are adorably and honestly humble. I respect what you've accomplished. I admire you."

But he didn't love her. He would never love her.

How sad that he could freely give her what she'd worked tirelessly to achieve, respect and admiration for her work, yet the one thing her heart craved from him was never to be. That realization gave her the strength to gently pull away from him and manage a smile.

"Thank you," she said.

This time he returned her smile with one that melted her heart and stirred longing deep in her. "Come. Let's celebrate tomorrow's pre-opening."

"Sure," she said, letting him lead her back to his room.

Letting him strip off their clothes and adore her body with his hands and mouth. Letting him do anything he wished with her.

No matter the outcome of her time with Luciano, she refused to deny herself a moment apart from him. Their separation would come far too soon anyway.

CHAPTER NINE

LUC STOOD AT the back of the banquet room, gaze fixed on Caprice behind the podium, a glass of the local cabernet franc caught between two fingers. He'd arrived late and missed the start of the ten-minute video of her program in action from initial therapy session to a patient hitting the slopes, but it was obvious her speech had kept the packed audience riveted. Now that the lights had come back up and she was explaining in more detail the benefits of her program, he had the pleasure of appreciating her beautiful mind and open heart.

Had he ever met a woman more giving? More caring of others? No. He'd realized that the moment he'd caught her working with Julian.

"At Caprice Tregore's, we promise therapy to fit your needs so you can ski free again," she said and paused as the applause swelled again, only dying down when she raised a hand begging silence. "Regardless of your degree of disability or ski experience, there is a program you can benefit from, stimulating mind and body. We welcome all of you with open arms, today, tomorrow and into the future. Thank you for coming and please enjoy the luncheon."

She nodded and backed away from the podium as applause went up a final time, growing in volume as the audience stood in her honor. Her smile grew too large and trembled, and even across the room he noted the glint of moisture in her eyes.

Her rush of emotion wasn't a surprise to him. No, what stunned him was the wad of anticipation lodged in his throat accompanied by a flutter in his gut, sensations he hadn't experienced since the first time he'd stepped into skis and shot down a mountain.

His heightened interest in her remained steady, but he knew it wouldn't last. The excitement never did, waning in months, weeks or sometimes days from each challenging sport he'd topped, coveted business deal he'd secured and desirable, aloof woman that he'd seduced.

These sensations he felt for Caprice would die as well. But could the same be said for her?

No. Though she'd never said it, he knew she believed herself in love with him. Her every touch, every look, conveyed what was in her heart.

He dragged in a breath and heard the crinkling of the message in his pocket, the paper that had been handed to him moments before the program started. Selfish bastard that he was, he thought of tossing it so everything would proceed as planned. He could keep Caprice by his side and in his bed for another week or more.

But he wouldn't do that to her. He'd hurt her too much. She must return to her life and he to his.

Her company would soar—he would make sure it did. She would find great success. One day she would find a good man, a thought he didn't like envisioning at this moment, maybe never would.

So be it. She would have a fine life and he would return to the one he'd chosen, one that didn't demand more of him than he was willing to give. It was the way it had to be.

He kept that thought in mind as the audience filed into the dining hall. No expenses had been spared for the selection of *antipasto misto*, *primo* of pastas, soup and risotto, *secondo* of meats and fish, *contorni* of vegetables and *insalata* and *dolce*, those being the first things some would select. Wines and mineral waters were in abundance as well.

Guests and prospective clients laughed and ate and drank and stole as much of Caprice's time as she'd allow. The new staff that she'd chosen remained busy booking appointments well into the next month, he suspected.

Everyone was happy, especially Caprice. She'd gotten the control she wanted, and he'd seen a new spark of life in his brother. That's why he'd hired her, and attaining his one goal should make him happy. So why wasn't he? Why was he gripped with the sensation that he was losing something he would never regain again?

"Congratulations, *bella*," he told Caprice a good hour later when she was finally free.

Excitement still danced in her eyes and kissed a rosy flush to her cheeks. Beautiful. She was absolutely beautiful.

She grasped his right hand and squeezed the fingers. "Never in my wildest dreams did I expect this wonderful response. You were so right about everything."

He saluted her with his *vino*. "Told you so."

Her grin shouted her happiness to the world as she accepted the champagne a waiter handed her. This was how he wished to remember her always.

Too soon she turned solemn. "What's wrong, Luciano? You look like you just lost your best friend."

He had, he admitted, taking a sip of the wine he favored and finding it bitter on his tongue, tainted by sour memories. "I'll tell you when this is over."

"Is it serious?" she asked, clear concern widening her eyes now.

He shook his head and managed the barest smile. "It

is good news for us. You're still much in demand. Smile," he told her as a young news reporter nabbed her attention.

It was the perfect cue for him to take his leave. In silence he retreated to his office. The amber silk tie went first with a shrug. Next he traded his cabernet for a generous glass of Bunnahabhain and slumped behind his desk, wanting to drown his irritation in Scotch.

Why couldn't he shake the feeling that he'd let the best thing in his life slip from his grasp forever?

The exhilarating high Caprice had floated on for the better part of two hours dropped her back to earth the second she stepped into Luciano's office. He sat at his desk, glass of amber liquid sitting before him either untouched or a refill. To the side was a clean glass beside the bottle of imported Scotch from the isle of Islay, a favored label of his.

"Forgive me but you don't look like a man who's received good news," she said.

One side of his mouth pulled up at the corner. "One man's good news is bad to another. Want a drink?"

"Am I going to need one?"

"Maybe." He upended the heavy glass, added two fingers of his imported Scotch and handed it to her.

She took the chair before his desk as well as the drink, struck with *déjà vu* of her very first meeting with him when she had just turned twenty and wanted desperately to be seen as a grown woman. That had been her first time drinking single-malt Scotch and dealing with an arrogant young champion. Both had been heady experiences she'd never forgotten.

"To you," he said, raising his glass.

She clinked her crystal to his, the clink clear and loud. "And you."

They each drank, hers a sip, his much more, then a spate of numbing silence.

A chill rippled through her, at odds with the whisky warming her tongue and throat. "Are you going to tell me this news?"

He nodded and cradled his glass between both palms, gaze lifting slowly to hers. "Mario is dead."

She blinked. "You're sure?"

He nodded. "Near dawn, a witness reported that Mario sped past their coupe on the A16, only to lose control. His Lamborghini shot over the stone wall of a viaduct and burst into flames on impact." He knocked back the remainder of his Scotch and grimaced, anyone's guess if the mouthful of liquor or distaste over the tragedy caused his expression. "It has taken an autopsy to determine Mario was behind the wheel."

"He's dead," she said. "He can't hurt me anymore."

"Correct." He pushed to his feet and paced the room. She massaged her temples, this day and everything that transpired happening far too fast for her to grasp. Or maybe the bit of alcohol had mixed unfavorably with the abundance of excitement.

He stood from his seat and walked to the view offered through the glass windows in his office. "With Mario dead, you can return to Colorado whenever you wish to. I will cover all expenses, as agreed to."

She caught the gasp that nearly burst free. He was setting her free. Giving her back the control over her life. She didn't have to remain in Italy under his protection a second longer. Not unless she wanted to.

And she did want to stay with Luciano. She didn't want this to end swiftly and so coldly. But every inch of him, from his body language to his words, made it clear he didn't share her view.

"Thank you for taking care of everything for me," she said in a surprisingly controlled tone that still made her tight throat ache. "I couldn't have done it without you."

She wouldn't cry. She wouldn't.

He frowned, tapping three fingers on the nearly floor-to-ceiling credenza. "I disagree. You are destined for greatness and would have achieved it with or without me. But I am glad, honored and grateful you agreed to work with me on the therapy pod."

"It was my pleasure," she said, painfully aware that was the only thing she could say because it was true. Being with him had been her pleasure and passion. Leaving was going to hurt for a long time.

He dropped in his chair and meted out another drink for them both, causing her to wonder when she'd drank all of hers. "To your continued success."

"And to yours," she said, retrieving her glass to join him in the toast.

Before all the past had tumbled out in a torrent of pain and confusion, she'd known that time would fly by in each other's arms. But to indulge in that now, even a kiss, would make their parting all the more heartbreaking. At least it would be that way for her.

She wanted to leave here the way she'd arrived. Chin up, determined to keep a careful distance from Luciano Duchelini.

"I'd better go now. There is so much I've left to do." She set her Scotch on the desk as she rose and started toward the door.

"Caprice," he said when she opened the door, and she steadied her nerves to look back at the most handsome man she'd ever met. "Would you join me for dinner tonight?"

She summoned up a polite smile. She'd been too nervous to eat much more than a few bites today, but all thought of food sickened her now in anticipation of their eventual parting. "I'd love to, but today is already packed. I have a meeting with the new staff now, and I want to find a flight out in the morning. Tonight I'll pack for the trip home."

His lips thinned, but he inclined his head once. "I'll arrange your transportation needs for you."

"Thank you." Did he have to sound too eager to see her off? She shook her head, refusing to show the pain this caused her, and told him the time.

She closed the door behind her and calmly strode through the outer office when every instinct in her begged her to run, to scream. If his PA noticed her state of distress, she held comment and continued sitting at her computer, diligently working.

Halfway down the hall Caprice gathered enough composure to return to the therapy pod. It took an hour to go over last-minute details with the staff. The pleasant surprise was seeing they'd received close to sixty applications for enrollment today and the phones were still ringing.

Success tasted sweet, but the sourness of heartbreak erased any pleasure. If she could just hold at bay the eventual breakdown of her emotions until she was away from her, until she was alone, she would be grateful.

Darkness had crept over the lodge by the time she found her suite. She'd no more than locked the door and kicked off her shoes when a knock came at the door.

She bit her lip, debating if she should ignore it. "Who is it?"

"Room service, Signorina Tregore."

A red flag waved before her eyes, but she fished several euros from her purse and opened the door. A smiling young man on the wait staff pushed a cart inside, the plate covered with a gleaming silver dome. Beside it sat one single yellow rose in a crystal vase.

"Shall I serve?" the waiter asked.

She shook her head and pressed the bills into his hands. "Thanks, but I'd rather wait awhile before I eat."

"Grazie!" he said with a bow and backed out the door.

A twist of the lock secured her privacy and a lift of the white drape over the table ensured there wasn't another surprise waiting for her there. The sealed white envelope on the cart stared back at her.

She knew before she broke the seal and pulled out the note that it was from Luciano, written in his bold, clearly read hand. "It is for the best this way. Luc."

Was it?

The note fell from her hands and her vision blurred. Pain knifed through her, drawing emotional blood. Yes, her mind agreed with him, but her heart wasn't buying it. Her heart wanted the man. Wanted his love.

Not to be.

She swiped at her eyes and took a long, hot shower, then packed everything but what she'd wear tomorrow. Exhausted, she fell into bed, the delivered dinner forgotten. If only she could just do the same with the imposing Italian she'd loved and clearly lost.

The wake-up call at seven gave Caprice the needed time to dress, secure her bags for the trip and leave her suite. One glance in the mirror confirmed that no amount of makeup could conceal the fact she'd had a fitful night's sleep.

She wrenched open the door and smothered a gasp. Luciano stood there, looking haggard as well.

His note flashed before her—*It is better this way.* So why was he here now?

She swallowed hard. "Is something wrong?"

He shook his head. "Not a thing that I'm aware of."

"Oh, good," she said, confused. "I trust everything is ready."

"To the minute." He glanced at his watch. "You are anxious to depart."

It was so tempting to refute that remark, but what was the point? She had to leave Italy and Luciano anyway. She had a ticket, lingering another hour or so threw that timetable off.

Even if she could easily leave at a later time, she still had to leave. Staying would only make it more difficult to walk away. And walk away she must.

"Allow me," he said, taking her bag from her.

"Thanks," she mumbled, closing the door behind her.

She trailed Luciano to the elevators and dreaded the ride down, secluded into close quarters with the man she would always love. And it was hell. More than anything she wanted to reach out to him. Touch him. Kiss him. But he stood like a Trojan, paying no attention to her at all.

After what seemed like forever, the elevator door whooshed open. He nodded for her to step out and she did, doing her best to pretend her nerves weren't scraped raw, that her insides weren't twisted into knots.

And then too quickly they were at the door with a private sedan waiting to whisk her to the airport, away from Italy. From the only man she would ever love.

This was what she'd wanted from the start. How could she complain if he didn't wish to accept her odd change of heart? He couldn't.

"Thank you," she said to Luc when they reached the door. "For everything."

And she meant it. His affection had given her back the confidence she hadn't realized she'd lacked. The incredible sex she'd been sure didn't exist. The faith he'd put in her as a businesswoman. The funds he'd given her to ensure she succeeded in her chosen field—not for a year but for decades, getting her over any foreseeable humps that may occur.

In short, he'd made sure she wouldn't need him ever again. Still, she was grateful. Everything he'd done for her was appreciated more than words could convey.

"It is I who should thank you for giving this opportunity to Julian." He smiled, though it was bittersweet to her eyes. "He seems excited."

"Julian will do fine. Tell him I'm just a phone call away if he needs to talk." And it took effort to not extend the same to Luc.

He nodded and crossed his strong arms over the muscled chest she'd loved to snuggle against. "I will. And please, if you discover you need anything more after you arrive at Tregore Lodge, just tell my assistant. She'll make sure you get it."

Not Luciano. No, he wouldn't want to hear from her once she stepped on that plane. When she left Italy and him.

"Goodbye," she said and slid into the backseat of the luxury sedan, not waiting for another clipped reply from him.

She wanted out of here, away from the temptation of going to him, of begging him to let her stay. That would never work. And if it did, it would be counterproductive to her forward progress.

By focusing on that thought, she endured the lengthy drive to the airport in silence. Once on the plane she asked the attendant for a sleeping aid and silently prayed that it would banish the insane desire to tell the pilot to turn the plane around and take her back to Luciano.

Her prayers were answered. When she awoke the next day, she was in Colorado. She was home, or an hour's drive from where she could watch the renovations of Tregore Lodge.

That alone made her deliriously happy. Or it should have. But she could barely manage a smile because she'd left something vital back in Italy. Her heart.

CHAPTER TEN

"You're an idiot," Julian said between breaks on the bench press Caprice had designed for upper-body strength and endurance.

For weeks, Luc had heard the same thing again and again, and he was tired of it. "Can't you think of anything else to say to me?"

Julian shrugged. "Nothing that makes me nearly as happy," he said, and resumed another set of reps, granting Luc a moment's peace.

Not that it would last long. Not that he was really complaining.

He'd gotten to where he enjoyed these early-morning workouts with Julian. It was like old times, save the fact his brother was using specialized equipment to suit his ability, and the unnerving fact that his brother was talking to him much more, though his favorite topic of late was to extol Caprice and her program at every opportunity.

Again, he couldn't complain or disagree. Julian had made remarkable recovery in such a short time, so much so that the old choking guilt that had held Luc responsible for the crippling accident had begun to wane. But it wouldn't totally go away, not when the ghosts from his past still hovered about, tossing kindling onto his guilt.

The memories of the accident continually scraped over

his emotional wounds, keeping them from healing. Being with Caprice and watching her personal struggle allowed him to realize that flaw in himself.

He'd seen firsthand the welcoming change in her once she'd unveiled the secrets that had emotionally chained her. It was time he came to grips with his past as well, accepting his guilt and moving beyond it.

"Next week Tregore Lodge hosts its grand opening," Julian said after finishing another impressive workout, his upper body gleaming with sweat, detailing muscles that hadn't been that well defined since the accident. "Do you plan to go?"

Luc stopped his tenth set of reps on the leg press and gaped at his brother. "I'm the last person she'd want to see there."

"Why would you think that? She loves you."

"Perhaps, but she deserves better than me."

"I was right the first time. You're an idiot." Julian shifted from the extra-wide bench he'd been on to his streamline wheelchair before an assistant could reach him, giving the wheel several hard pushes that jetted him across the room.

"Julian," Luc shouted and his brother stopped and stared at him, his heart in his mouth for what he was about to say. "I'm sorry. So damned sorry."

His brother wheeled to face him, frown deepening. "For what?"

Luc waved a hand in the air, the movement ponderous under the mountain of guilt he carried. "You wouldn't be bound to a wheelchair if I hadn't goaded you into that race. I know you looked back at me out of concern, and that's why you lost your edge and fell."

"You can't believe that."

"It's the truth," he said, the admission taking a long time to sort out. "I was out to prove I could be as reckless as you, but where your bravado was based on talent, mine was driven by guilt."

Julian sent the chair wheeling back to his brother. "Don't think that way. I wanted to best you in that race because you were the best in Alpine, winning medal after medal. And for the record, I didn't look back out of worry but relief. With you down, the win was in the bag. I took my mind and eyes off the game and that split-second error is why I'm resigned to a wheelchair for life. Got it?"

Luc let that sink in, feeling some of the weight lift from him in the process. "Got it."

"Good." Julian left again, but stopped at the opening to the massage pod, balancing his chair on its rear wheels and pivoting to face Luc. "It is not your fault that our family is dysfunctional. We are capable of making our own decisions. If they were bad ones, it is our own fault."

This time Luc cracked a smile. "You're pretty smart for a little brother."

"About time you realized that," Julian teased. "Have I told you lately you are a complete, utter ass for sending Caprice away?"

"That was your parting remark last night, brother," Luc said, resuming his reps with renewed vigor despite the pain of stretching the injured muscle in his leg. He was driven by anger at himself as he allowed that utilizing Caprice's program might help him improve physically.

Julian set his chair right and pushed through the opening. "Excellent," he shouted. "I don't want you to forget."

As if that were even possible.

Luc did two more reps, then stopped cold, realization slamming into him with the force of a lightning bolt. His brother was right.

He was an ass. A terrified one.

For years he'd carried the responsibility of all that had

gone wrong with those he'd loved on his broad shoulders, convinced that was his burden to bear for life. But Julian had just opened his eyes to the truth.

It had taken him years to see that closing his eyes to his wife's infidelity would have saved her life then, but it wouldn't guarantee the same wouldn't happen in the future. Chances were she would have left him at the first opportunity. Her death wasn't his fault.

Just as it wasn't totally his fault that Julian was disabled for life.

It was a hard admission to make, but it was the truth he'd avoided for years, preferring to use his failed attempts at therapy as his excuse to drop out of competition completely. He'd used guilt as the reason to hide from life. To avoid any emotional entanglement with a woman.

Yes, his recovery had been painful, but other skiers with far worse injuries had pushed themselves until they were back on the slopes. None of them had chosen the coward's way out.

But fear had consumed him, destroying the exhilarating challenge of mastering the mountain again. Not fear of losing, but of winning because he no longer believed he deserved it. Just like he'd convinced himself all women were after him for his money.

So he'd thrown himself into unbelievable challenges in the corporate world, but inside he was little more than a robot, a shell of a man, performing the role of ex-champion playboy without emotion. He hadn't realized how shallow and lonely his life had been until Caprice had come back into it, and even then he'd denied himself the true pleasure just being with her gave him.

Caprice. His chest tightened and his sex stirred at the mere thought of her. But it was the warmth in his chest— *his heart!*—that brought him to his knees.

Julian was right. He was an idiot.

Caprice was unlike any woman he'd ever met, challenging him on more levels than he'd believed possible, challenging him to look at the deeper part of himself that he'd hidden from.

But he'd resisted searching his soul until now and had totally refused to open his heart, so certain that doing so would cause him heartache instead of joy.

And oddly it did just that now.

He ached for Caprice. Wanted her. But by realizing that he wasn't the bad guy, that he did deserve happiness this late, he'd remained the taciturn machine and had driven her away. He'd let his guilt prevent him from opening his heart to her.

Now he was ready to do just that. But was she lost to him? Did he stand a chance?

He had no idea.

The only thing glaringly clear was the fact he couldn't let his relationship with Caprice end this way. He couldn't bear the thought of living without her, even though the prospect of giving his heart to her scared the hell out of him. It terrified him more to think of living like this— without her, without love.

Luc swung to his feet and stalked to his suite. He had one chance to make this right with her. This was the most challenging run of his life and for the first time in years he was ready to do whatever it took to win.

It took an entire month and one week before she could move back into the lodge.

She stood in the spacious foyer, turning a slow circle, in awe of the changes. Luciano had given her the plans to okay, but she'd never dreamed it would be so massive. So dominating a force perched on this ledge surrounded by

denuded slopes where old pistes were being cleared while
new alternative slopes for beginners were being formed. It
was, in short, a miracle—a work of art, from the towering
vaulted ceilings to a fireplace whose red stones took up a
wall yet didn't overpower the massive room with heavy
crossbeams.

All things she'd envisioned in the scant future. Luciano's largesse had made it all come true.

"Welcome home."

"Karla?" Caprice asked upon hearing that voice from
her past, whirling to the friend she hadn't seen since high
school to embrace her, ensuring she wasn't dreaming.
"What? Why are you here?"

Her free-spirited friend laughed. "Luciano hired me the
day I applied for the position of counselor."

"I had no idea."

About very little it seemed.

Throughout her stay in Italy, she'd been given updates
on the progress in Colorado and asked for her signature
regarding legal issues on the employment of "key staff,"
as he'd put it. She'd been too involved establishing the
program at his lodge and dealing with her own conflict-
ing emotions over him to pay close attention to what she
signed.

Not good business sense at all and she wasn't proud of
that admission.

Just how deeply had he dug into her past? Certainly
enough to know that she'd been close friends with Karla.
That her friend had been interviewed by Luciano—that
he'd handpicked a women who'd befriended her when she'd
needed it most. "You must be perfect for the position," she
said and embraced Karla, "because Luciano is extremely
particular about his employees and mine."

Karla laughed and gave her a friendly squeeze before

backing away. "Don't I know it! Hey, for what it's worth he raved about your fantastic program. If I didn't know better I would have sworn it was his baby."

His baby...

The thought of having Luciano's child fizzed through her blood like champagne, leaving her heady and wistful and yet sad. Her time had visited her on the flight back. There would be no baby in her near future.

Caprice shook off the odd melancholy with a smile. "Luciano has a vested interest in Tregore Lodge, so in a way it is his baby. And I don't mean to be rude," she added, "but I've had a long day finishing details on my therapy unit and need to get some rest."

"Say no more," Karla said. "We'll catch up later."

"Great!"

Caprice considered it good luck that she made the long walk from the front desk to fetch a key to her rooms without further delay. Sleep. She just wanted to bury her head under the blankets and let this hurt pass her by.

But when she awoke the next morning at 4:00 a.m., she knew quality rest wasn't in her future. Luciano had tormented her dreams, just as he'd managed to infiltrate those idle moments of her mind during the day while she was in Italy.

Would it ever stop?

It had to. She had to get a grip and move full speed on her lodge—the lodge that he'd poured more than a million dollars into for renovation. But even then, this program wasn't his baby, it was hers.

Now was the time to prove that.

Two weeks later she was settled and moving forward with establishing her program here, but nowhere close to feeling settled in her personal life. She missed Luciano. Far too often she'd caught herself reaching for him at night.

She had to snap out of it now. Somehow Luciano had moved heaven and earth to have the mountain and surrounding grounds well groomed before the first snow. Though that was months away yet, she would receive patients for the therapy unit before fall.

That gave her three weeks to have the interior finished and the staff totally ready to perform at top speed. Long, tiring hours were needed with her having a clear head focused on business. It would have been a snap to achieve eight weeks ago. Now?

She took a breath, held it and blew it out in a long, trembling rush. At this moment she struggled to find any peace of mind. Struggled harder to focus on anything besides the man she'd left in Italy, the same man who had made her dreams come true here only to break her heart.

It was maddening that she longed for him still and she hated herself for it. She'd known going in that it wasn't going to last. It couldn't last. She didn't want it. Didn't seek it. So why couldn't she let it go?

Her cell rang, or more precisely broke into song, a sound she hadn't heard in weeks while she was abroad. She checked the displayed number but didn't recognize it.

"Hello," she said after the sixth ring.

"Caprice, darling, how are you?" came a feminine voice she hadn't heard in decades.

She shook her head. Was she hallucinating? Her mother? Calling her now?

"Caprice?" her mother asked again.

Her stomach curdled. The last person she wished to engage in even the briefest of conversations was her mother.

Caprice dropped onto her bed. "I'm here."

"Oh, thank goodness," her mother said, not the least

deterred by her daughter's abruptness. "The baron and I just bumped into your Italian and discovered you'd been his guest in the Alps for a month. Is it true?"

She shook her head, always knowing her mother would call the moment she learned her daughter was involved with a billionaire. "Yes, Mother."

"Well, good. I was afraid to hope you were having an affair with a rich man."

"We're not involved," she said.

"Splendid. Darling, take my advice and choose a man with a title and not some sports medal. A woman never goes wrong attached to nobility."

"I'll bear that in mind." She bit her lower lip and gripped the phone, gathering strength to warn her mother about her upcoming announcement. "Mother, I'm giving a press conference tomorrow—"

"Oh, sorry to cut this short, darling, but the baron says it's time to leave. We're off to Brazil for Carnival. Do smile when you meet the press. Ta-ta."

"Right," Caprice said to a suddenly dead line that ended another typical out-of-the-blue call from her mother.

That was her mother, more concerned about how Caprice would look than what she planned to say. But then if her mother had known what she had prepared, she might have tried to change her mind.

That wasn't going to happen. It couldn't, she thought as she paced her office.

Where had her mother run into Luciano? And why was she letting him occupy her thoughts? Wasn't she nervous enough over the upcoming press conference? Stressed and terrified over what reaction she would receive from her friends and strangers?

As for forewarning her mother, she likely wouldn't have

believed Caprice was attacked, and she certainly wouldn't have wanted the world to know about it.

But Caprice knew she had to reveal the truth, the whole ugly mess, in hopes other woman would pay better heed to their own vulnerability.

In that regard, Luciano had been right. She realized it now. Knew she couldn't hide behind silence any longer, even though she no longer had to fear Mario's retribution.

God, she never should have feared that for years. That error in judgment had vindicated Mario and sentenced her into shamed silence.

That was the one thing she wanted to make sure never happened to another woman. Rape and abuse had to be reported or the victims were sentenced to suffer in silence.

Tomorrow was opening day at Tregore Lodge and she would stay up all night to ensure everything was ready. She desperately needed this premiere to go as smoothly as the one in Italy had. But at Luciano's lodge, she'd had his support and staff at her beck and call.

Her opening wasn't as grand or nearly as organized, despite the fact that his crew had done a remarkable job rebuilding the lodge. The timing was crucial. She had competition, and getting the word out that she was here and ready for both adaptive and standard skiers was vital. She had sent grand opening invitations to all the news stations covering the areas around Colorado Springs, Denver and Loveland, touting the merits of her program and mentioning that a sister facility resided in Italy under the direction of former champion Julian Duchelini.

She was smart enough to realize that name alone could draw skiers to her facility. Plus, having Julian make a surprise appearance tomorrow would make a massive difference. But what would he think of her announcement?

She couldn't fret about that now!

Tomorrow was enough to worry about. She had to wow the press and potential clients now or she stood a chance of failing. And she had to unburden her soul of the rape.

Her future as a whole person depended upon her nailing both points.

Luc slipped in the door of Tregore Lodge and took a position along the side of the great hall, pleased by the crowd gathering for Caprice's grand opening. He looked beyond the attendees to the beauty and integrity of the structure and furnishings and nodded, noting with pleasure the attention paid to detail, right down to the new mantel gracing the massive fireplace.

The entire lodge was impressively massive. Upbeat. Yet a touch of rustic appeal vibrated through it like a favored song, which was exactly what Caprice had wanted and he'd balked at, confident that a departure from original would look far better.

He'd been wrong, much to his surprise.

Now, as he scanned the people gathering for the grand opening, he was confident Tregore Lodge and her program would be a huge success. He threaded his fingers through his hair, fully aware she didn't need him or any man now.

But did she at least still want him?

He'd soon find out.

Luc slipped from the crowd and made his way to Caprice's office, wanting to catch her before she met with the press, wanting to see her, hold her, kiss her. He wanted her, and he knew exactly how he was going to win her over this time. Permanently.

"Mr. Duchelini!" Her secretary popped up from her chair, her frantic gaze flitting from him to the closed office door.

He pointed to Caprice's office. "Is she in there?"

The secretary wrung her hands. "Yes, but I don't think you should go— Wait! You can't do that!"

But he was already through the door and closing it behind him, or trying to with the secretary fast on his heels. He stopped, his hungry gaze arrested by the sight of Caprice digging through the mountain of papers on her desk, looking harried and desirable.

"Do you need something?" she asked, not looking up.

"Mr. Duchelini is here," the secretary said, shooting him a scolding look. "Luciano Duchelini."

Caprice jerked upright and stared at him, and the pain and worry in her eyes tore at something buried inside him he hadn't known existed. "Why are you here?"

"Julian asked me to come," he said. "He caught a head cold that quickly infected his lungs. His physician advised him not to attempt the trip. He sends his regrets along with me."

The lips he hungered for pursed. "Fine. Now if you'll excuse me—"

"I need to talk with you alone first."

She looked up again, and this time he saw a mounting sense of urgency spark in her eyes. "Sorry. We go live in five minutes."

And with that she ran out the door, leaving him standing there like a fool. A rejected fool. With good reason, he realized as he stalked to the door to take his leave.

He stopped dead in his tracks, hand on the brass knob. He'd accused her of running away from him and her feelings, but he'd been guilty of doing the same thing.

Luc shook his head, finding it ironic that it had taken losing Caprice for him to finally rip his blinders off. He wasn't backing down or away again.

He trailed her to the great room, followed her onto the dais and took up a stance at the side behind the curtain, but the sudden flash of cameras en route proved many in the audience recognized him. So be it if this moment was recorded forever. Whatever the outcome, it would certainly leave an indelible mark on his memory and his future.

"Thank you all for coming," Caprice began. "If I could direct your attention to the screen above the hearth, we'll run a short video depicting my program."

She moved to the opposite side of the dais, where a chair had been positioned for her behind a small curtain. Her gaze flitted once to his before the lights dimmed and the same video that had played at his grand opening began.

As soon as the ten-minute video ended, the lights came on and Caprice returned to the podium to give the same abbreviated speech. Lines of stress radiated from her eyes and mouth, and her stance was noticeably stiffer.

Luc frowned, alert to the rising sense of urgency Caprice projected.

"Any questions?" she asked.

"Is Luciano Duchelini involved in the day-to-day running of Tregore Lodge or is he just your backer?" a reporter asked.

She fidgeted with her notes. "My business association with la Duchi is not on the agenda for discussion. Next question," she said, pointing to another person.

The next twenty minutes she fielded random questions about the renovations and her program. "Any more?" she asked, allowing an overly long pause.

She took a deep breath and heaved it out, and Luc did the same, feeling the tension roiling through her, fearful what had upset her so. "There's one more thing I wish to touch on here. Take notes because I won't be answering questions at this time."

Luc was on the dais and by her side in an instant, hearing the strain in her voice and fearing she was close to losing control. "What's wrong?"

"You'll find out in a moment," she whispered with a faint smile before sobering and facing the audience again. Luc stepped back out of the limelight, giving her the stage.

"I wish to address this to all women in hopes it will keep another woman from living with the torment I have," she said, her voice surprisingly strong and clear now. "Seven years ago I was the victim of a rape. Out of fear, humiliation and worry I kept that dark secret."

She paused when the audience murmured among themselves, waiting for them to quiet. "I don't know if he attacked other women, and because he has since died I won't reveal his name. But I urge any woman who has been victimized to step forward immediately and seek help. Don't let one act of violence victimize you for life."

She stepped back, and he noted the barest tremble shake through her then and the audience stared at her in stark silence.

Luc stepped forward, faced Caprice and began clapping. Soon others joined in until the room exploded with applause.

"Thank you," she said once more as she stepped to the mic. Then with a bow, she reached for his hand and he escorted her back to the privacy of her office.

"That was extremely courageous of you," he said.

She shrugged. "It had to be said."

"I agree," he said, uncertain how to begin something so vital when his senses were on overload just being so near her again. "I'm very proud of you."

She glanced up at him and flushed a lovely pink, a nervous smile playing over the lips he longed to claim. "Thanks. Is there something you needed?"

Just the opening he needed. "Yes, you. Come back to Italy with me."

She stiffened. "I have a business to run."

"You could do that from Italy."

She slapped her palms flat on her desk. "I won't be your mistress, Luciano."

He nudged her chin up despite her attempt to pull away from him. "I wouldn't dream of asking that of you. My God, Caprice, I love you deeply. I want you with me. Is that so hard to understand?"

"What did you say?" Caprice sputtered.

"*Bella*, you are my world. My present. My future. I never realized what love was until you opened your heart to me." And as tears slipped from her eyes, he came around her desk and dropped onto one knee, his gaze riveted on the strong woman before him. "I love you, Caprice Tregore. You have stolen my heart, and I am nothing without you."

"I love you, too," she said, stepping closer to him, both trembling hands resting on his shoulders now.

In a blink her world narrowed to this moment. This man. This door opening to the future she'd dreamed of having and feared would never come about.

Luc smiled, his spirits lightening, realizing he was actually happy. The fear, the apprehension vanished. Absolutely nothing in his life had ever felt so right. So freeing. So perfect. Not the competitions that had challenged his mind and body on the slopes. Not the conquests he'd made in business or pleasure.

This was real and he wanted it. Wanted her, now and forever. "Marry me, Caprice. Make me a happy man."

"You're serious," she said, half sobbing, half laughing. "You really want a marriage with a house and children and a forever kind of love?"

"Yes, I want a real marriage with you as well as children

to start the next generations of Duchelini champions," he said with a grin. "Your answer?"

She choked out a sob, fingers pressed to her lips, and then slowly gifted him with a smile that made his heart swell with love he'd denied entrance to for years. "Yes," she said, tugging him up into her open arms. "Yes."

He raised one brow, holding her close. "How about tomorrow?"

"It's a date," she said.

They chose the closest spot, flying out that night for Vegas to become husband and wife the next morning, photos taken of the kiss sealing their commitment at Tregore Lodge splashed on all the gossip magazines and newspapers.

"No regrets?" she asked her new husband the second morning of their marriage.

"Only one," he said, pulling her luscious naked body against his, smiling to find her wet and ready for him again. "We waited too long."

"You'll get no argument from me," she said, kissing his chest, his chin before settling in for a long lusty kiss that left them breathless, prolonging the passion as long as they could.

"Let's keep it that way," he said, and surrendered to the sizzling passion they had found in each other's arms.

* * * * *

A sneaky peek at next month...

MODERN™

POWER, PASSION AND IRRESISTIBLE TEMPTATION

My wish list for next month's titles...

In stores from 18th July 2014:

☐ Zarif's Convenient Queen — Lynne Graham

☐ His Forbidden Diamond — Susan Stephens

☐ The Argentinian's Demand — Cathy Williams

☐ The Ultimate Seduction — Dani Collins

In stores from 1st August 2014:

☐ Uncovering Her Nine Month Secret — Jennie Lucas

☐ Undone by the Sultan's Touch — Caitlin Crews

☐ Taming the Notorious Sicilian — Michelle Smart

☐ His by Design — Dani Wade

Available at WHSmith, Tesco, Asda, Eason, Amazon and Apple

Just can't wait?

Visit us Online

You can buy our books online a month before they hit the shops! **www.millsandboon.co.uk**

0714/01

 *Special Offers*

Every month we put together collections and longer reads written by your favourite authors.

Here are some of next month's highlights— and don't miss our fabulous discount online!

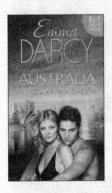

On sale 18th July

On sale 18th July

On sale 18th July

Save 20%
on all Special Releases

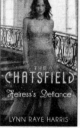

Join our *EXCLUSIVE* eBook club

FROM JUST £1.99 A MONTH!

Never miss a book again with our hassle-free eBook subscription.

★ Pick how many titles you want from each series with our flexible subscription

★ Your titles are delivered to your device on the first of every month

★ Zero risk, zero obligation!

There really is nothing standing in the way of you and your favourite books!

Start your eBook subscription today at www.millsandboon.co.uk/subscribe

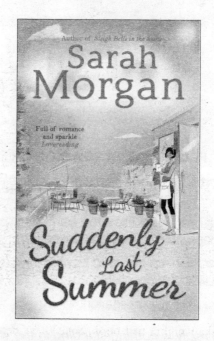

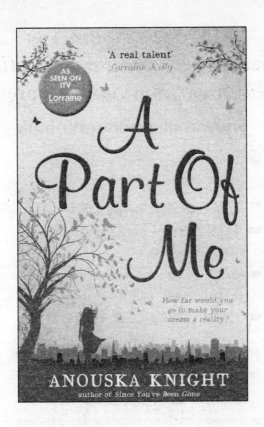

Anouska Knight's first book, *Since You've Been Gone*, was a smash hit and crowned the winner of Lorraine's Racy Reads. Anouska returns with *A Part of Me*, which is one not to be missed!

Get your copy today at:
www.millsandboon.co.uk

Discover more romance at

www.millsandboon.co.uk

- ❤ WIN great prizes in our exclusive competitions
- ❤ BUY new titles before they hit the shop.
- ❤ BROWSE new books and REVIEW your favourites
- ❤ SAVE on new books with the Mills & Boon® Bookclub™
- ❤ DISCOVER new authors

PLUS, to chat about your favourite reads, get the latest news and find special offers:

- 📘 Find us on facebook.com/millsandboon
- 🐦 Follow us on twitter.com/millsandboonuk
- ❤ Sign up to our newsletter at millsandboon.co.uk